CLACKAMAS LITERARY REVIEW

2018
Volume XXII

Clackamas Community College
Oregon City, Oregon

CLACKAMAS LITERARY REVIEW

Managing Editor
Matthew Warren

Associate Editors

Jennifer Davis	Trevor Dodge	Jack Eikrem
Victoria Marinelli	Delilah Martinez	Nicole Rosevear
	Amy Warren	

Assistant Editors & Designers

Kehau Aipolani	Nathan Bas	LeeAnn Campbell
Jordan Hammock	Patrick David Hanson	Masen Hopkins
Rachael Lane-Stedman	Trina Lockard	Jeffrey Lowry
Theresa L. Malley	Ali Noman	Patricia Payne
Abigael Santiago	Caitlynne Schuebel	Sara Sklenicka
Jacob D. Thompson	Hollyn Walston	

Cover Art
The Reader by Nate Orton

The Clackamas Literary Review is published annually at Clackamas Community College. Manuscripts are read from September 1st to December 31st. By submitting your work to *CLR*, you indicate your consent for us to publish accepted work in print and online. Issues I–XI are available through our website; issues XII–XXI are available on our Submittable, and through your favorite online bookseller.

Clackamas Literary Review
19600 Molalla Avenue, Oregon City, Oregon 97045
ISBN: 978-1-7320333-0-6
Printed by Lightning Source
www.clackamasliteraryreview.org

CONTENTS

PROSE

CONTRIBUTORS

Editors' Note

Strangers. That is who we are to one another. So often unaware of the passersby whose lives are as rich and complex and hopeful and tragic as our own, we look down, around; past and through. We disconnect—blind to the other while lost in the self. And yet here we are, meeting by way of words on a page, seeing—perhaps for the first time—our own lives reflected in the stories of others. And that is why we publish the *Clackamas Literary Review*—to introduce writers and poets to their readers.

For more than twenty years, the *CLR* has welcomed storytellers from around the world to share experiences and emotions both universal and unique—to bring to readers human stories, those that remind us just how we are the same, *especially* when we are different. Our work as editors is to publish such writing.

This volume shows us that the unfamiliar is only what we have not yet experienced, that when reading the stories of others we become aware, we see, we connect—we are no longer strangers.

The Morning after the Revolution

John Sibley Williams

The world comes all at once. Some
vagueness humming in the outlying
dark arranges into song. Silhouettes
adopt form, which we name, label,
& eventually learn to scorn. A light
breaks through this canopy of fog &
roof, falls into our hands, where we
can safely snuff it out. I've spent so
long gaging distances between stars
I cannot discern love from broken
promises. My city sprawls naked &
sinister, & without regret I ask it for
more of the same. A body thunders
into another: a kind of violence that
resembles sex, which looks a hell of
a lot like prayer, which is a tool we
pull from its shelf when we cannot
piece ourselves back together. I can-
not piece myself back together. Son,
I'm sorry for the way things turned
out. Just know the colors the clouds
adopt this morning aren't their own.

Learning to Speak

Pat Anthony

Write they said, of childhood and so I
wrote about the dark passage where

      there was no waystation, just some
          crashing into uncertainty

like the way the bike collided with the
unforgiving hurricane fence on that first

      ride through the grassy yard crumpling the blue
          the turquoise blue front fender shattering

so much more than the headlight. No other
kids witnessed my disgrace since an unbreakable

      rule meant there could be no playing
          with neighbor kids even when

I got a volleyball a year later
to improve my posture she said

to throw it on the roof and be sure
    to tell the gym teacher how

much I practiced fighting the folds of the long
housedress I soon grew to hate the dying

    thump of ball on gravelly grass
      sure that everyone pulling up

to the stop sign for Oak Street
had to see and snicker

    I hurled it then into the back of the toolshed
      to deflate without having to take a nail to it.

    If childhood was an adventure
      how to explain that

it occurred inside a dark tunnel always
narrowing, no light, but I could count

    on the surety of the whistle
      the onslaught of the train

its roaring engine
grown accustomed like some small puppy

    conditioned to the can opener's whirr
      to say again and again how I liked alone.

Of her small, corrupt body

Line taken from The Big Sleep

Kathleen Hellen

Isn't she smooth? somebody said
when, overlooking the camera
she couldn't tell
(anyone) her legs
like shapeless shadow
opening to auditions
straddling the scripted
silence, what really
happened when
extortion (blacklist)
flickered, watching it and
watching it (again?) when
object/objects lost focus
when spotlight plotted
skin (pornographer?)
Isn't she smooth? somebody said

The Good Teacher

Jack Donahue

My little body flew at the crack of his bat,
a solid shot to the skull,
home run bouncing off the furthest wall.
Check his head the surgeon said,
get him fitted for an ear.

Here, here! Sign him!
Sign him! Up! Up!
Can you smell this?
Can you taste that?

What is this letter?
What was that sound?
Cover your eyes. Cover your eyes!
Now open your eyes.
Watch my mouth.
Read this word.

I see this word
but do not hear him.
Are there any senses left

another doctor said,
yes, yes, he can still feel.

Then hit him again she said,
he said, they all said
better teach him how not to cry.

"I Will Try"

Akachi Obijiaku

As my fingers peel to reveal my raw and tender flesh
And I squirm for the souls of my broken nails
I wonder where all the mechanical wonders are
Praised an innovation—attacked as a threat

I ponder the hopelessness of my human capital
Scraping pots and pans, condemned to listen to petty banter
The things they got me doing in this kitchen
Will deliver me canker sores by nightfall

Scared to touch my baby boy
He, wagering whether to confront me
Ask me what happened to the girl he fell in love with
The one who didn't return every night stinking of spoilt beans

And I will try
I will try to remember her
Remember my old life—how comfortable I once was

But looking down at my broken palms,
I shall fail—slowly, most likely, defensively
And wrap my blisters up, to heal quick for the next day

C9

Simon Perchik

Before it could endure its undertow your skull
hardened, was silenced with its marrow
kept calm by the half once seawater

and the other taking longer
though everything makes a sound
gathers you in, the way rust on all sides

scratches—with both hands you comb your hair
as if it still smells from a gate
that's no longer iron down the middle

and there you listen to it opening
—from both sides reaching out for air
that sounds like shoreline, further and further.

Attack

S.W. Campbell

All of the muscles on my body are tense, ready to spring into action at a moment's notice. My shoulders rise higher than normal, an attempt to make myself look bigger, a leftover trait from our species' primal past. The energy courses through my body making the hair on the back of my neck and arms stand on end. My heart pounds in my chest, my breath, normal, feels rapid and uncontrolled. I'm on the edge, and I am scared to death of falling off.

"Welcome to Subway, how may I help you sir?"

"A six-inch meatball sub please." I mumble my reply. My voice, normally booming and filled with confidence, is quiet in my own head. Barely perceptible to those around me.

"What was that sir?" The worker behind the counter leans forward, hoping that the closer distance will aid him in hearing my stifled words.

"A six-inch meatball sub on white please." I say it a little louder. He seems to hear me this time, but my voice sounds far away in my own ears.

I meet the eye of the man standing behind the counter, but only briefly. The eyes are the window to the soul. I don't want people looking into my soul right now. I don't want them to see the anxiety and the fear. My foot begins to tap a quick rhythm as I watch my sandwich being made, a quick percussive beat on the tile floor. My muscles will not loosen, if anything they tighten further. I will my foot to stop, my shoulders to lower, my body to relax. They obey me for a second, but as soon as my mind moves on to another thought, my shoulders begin to rise again. The fibers of muscles pull taut.

The making of the sandwich is a step-by-step process. Each step requires a question and an answer. With each answer I feel the need to look at the man behind the counter. I avoid looking him in the eye. I look at his nose, at his ear, at his mouth. Anything to avoid direct contact.

"Cheese?"

"Swiss."

"Toasted?"

"No."

"Toppings?"

"Black olives, mayonnaise, and red wine vinegar."

"Did you say pickles?"

"No."

Whenever I don't have to talk to him I look away. I look at the pictures of food on the wall above him. I look down at his hands preparing the sandwich as I give my directions. I look briefly at the other workers and those around me. Sometimes my eyes come to rest for brief moments, distracted, but only for a second. Sometimes I stare at those around me, the workers or my fellow customers, letting my eyes watch them at their work. The connection of watching someone is somehow soothing. When they feel me watching and look up, I quickly look away.

As I move forward along the sandwich assembly line I re-tuck in my shirt for the fourth time since I've walked in. I'm hypersensitive, every little piece that is out of place must be fixed. A nervous tick, a sign of someone who is having difficulty. I want to scream. I want to rip off my shirt and run around like an idiot. I feel like I am about to explode. How can nobody notice this? They have to be able to notice. I can feel my skin literally buzzing with energy.

I reach forward to grab a bag of chips. I finger the packaging on the rack for a second before changing my mind and grabbing a different brand. I can feel people watching my every movement, feel them judging me. Look at that man. What the hell is wrong with him? He looks like a nervous wreck. Settle down fella. Just relax. What a basket case. I am the only member of the audience to my little drama, but it feels as though all eyes are upon me.

My heart's pace quickens more. I reach up and clutch my chest for a moment like I'm having a heart attack. A silly notion. I am as healthy as a horse. My mind and body are ready, waiting for the attack, waiting for the lion to leap out of the bushes to maul me. It is going to leap at any moment, my mind and body are convinced of it. Adrenaline courses through my veins in anticipation. I try to slow my breathing. I only have to survive this social savannah for a bit more.

I get to the register and open my wallet. My hands, normally steady and sure, are clumsy. I try to pull out seven dollars, two ones and a five, but it takes twice as long as normal. It's as though the hands picking through the wallet aren't mine. It's as though I'm controlling a robotic hand from a long distance away, watching via a camera with a long delay. Every command has to be several seconds ahead of the actual movement. I fumble through my wallet and pull out too much money. I use the back of my hand to press my wallet against my chest so I can use all of my fingers to clumsily separate out the extra bills.

The man behind the counter waits patiently. He is in no hurry. I feel like I'm being rushed. The lion is getting closer. I can sense him hiding somewhere nearby. He is crouching and ready to spring. I hand the man the money and he hands me back my change. I grab my sandwich and shove the change in my pocket, a quarter escaping and falling onto the floor. I reach down quickly to grab it, my body shaking and my face red with embarrassment. My first attempt fails, as does my second. I cannot get my fingernails under it, they are ragged and bitten. Please, come on, this is torment. The third attempt does the trick, I stand up and put the quarter in my pocket.

The man behind the counter smiles at me. I look back at the other waiting customers. Some faces are bored. Some faces are smiling at hidden thoughts. Some faces are mad and impatient at the added wait. Little worlds separated by space and the inability to communicate. I desperately want one to break through the divide. I desperately want to look one in the eye and feel a connection. I desperately want one to step forward to reassure me, tell me everything is going to be fine. All of the eyes are blank, all of the windows are opaque. I have to tell myself everything will be fine. My only advisor is someone I don't completely trust right now.

I walk hurriedly from the fast food eatery. My motions feel jerky and unnatural, as though my joints are held together by overly tightened rubber bands. Past the people eating at the tables. Some alone and some with company. Some smiling and laughing. Some looking bored and weary. I can feel the hot breath of the lion on my neck. I can feel the wetness of my shirt at the small of my back and in my armpits. I escape out the door to safety. The lion falls behind. It is safer here. Safer outside. Here the private worlds around me are more spread out.

My furtive motions carry me back to my office. As I cross the bridge over the railroad tracks a quiet little voice tells me to jump over the railing. The logical part of my mind instantly pushes the thought back and for a second a very real fear of falling comes over me. It is an instant, just an instant. An instant where the tiny little voice had me convinced. I am not suicidal. I do not want to die. I want to live. It's not a want to die that makes me think about jumping over the railing and falling the three stories to the railroad tracks below. It is only a desperate need to make something happen. It feels like something is going to happen. Waiting for something to happen is driving me insane. Maybe if something happens I won't feel like this anymore. Something. Anything.

I arrive at my building and get in the elevator with a woman who wears too much perfume. I want to yell at her to stop wearing so much perfume, that she has overdosed on her cure and it has become a poison. I worry that she can see the sheen of sweat across my brow, suspicious on a cold day. She gets off first, but her overpowering scent remains, a companion for the rest of my elevated journey. I breathe through my mouth. I get off the elevator and the distraction is gone, my thoughts turn back to myself. A few more steps. Open and close the door. Make a friendly remark to the secretary. Walk into my office. Close the door behind me. Sit down in my chair.

I stare at the wall in front of me. My body is motionless but my mind is an unstoppable machine of perpetual motion. It's just an anxiety attack. Just wait. It will pass. This isn't permanent. Just wait. Don't worry. Just breathe. My body and subconscious scream at me, calling the soothing voice a liar. You will always be this way. There is no escape. You are insane. You will never feel normal again. It is only a matter of time. I breathe deep and slow. In and out. I push the negative thoughts away. It's okay. Your body and brain are lying to you. They are just muscles having knee jerk reactions. These are battles you have fought before. You don't have to worry. You don't have to be scared. Just ride it out. You'll see.

I sit at my desk and shake, breathing deeply, repeating a sooth-ing mantra in my head. This is not who I am, this is only temporary, this is not who I am, this is only temporary. I don't have to hide, I don't have to be afraid. The vibrations beneath my skin settle, my breath begins slowing and I feel some of the tension in my muscles ease. I am not relaxed, but I am at least looser. I have escaped again, I have made it through again. I unwrap my sandwich and open up a comedy website on my computer. I concentrate on the task at hand, one step at a time. The thoughts that set me off remain, but I ignore them, shove them back where they are out of the way. It's over. It's passed. There's a voice in the back of my head that I do my best to ignore. For how long?

Galaxy Observations and Reports to the Contrary

Stephen R. Roberts

Studies disclose the universe should not actually exist.
Some may feel the same about this particular poem.
Each contains a number of particles and anti-particles
that will annihilate one another if they come in contact.

If there's a scale to measure what remains when words
and non-words collide, it will show nothing's left over
but the poem shimmering in a mirror of dark energy.
Observations between matter and anti-matter matter.

Adverbs and adjectives often bounce around erratically
like arthritically challenged squid or late grasshoppers.
When they crash, they fall onto a page of white sky
in disarray, legs kicking every direction, until negated.

Since exotic dark matter exists in certain galaxy clusters,
and goes naked in front of windows with the blinds up,
we feel dark energy tingling deliciously along our spines.
For every person who reads this poem, ten others will not.

Further studies of the subject could reverse all findings.
Humankind could be misinformed of our prominence

in the big scheme of things, a wobbling galaxy cluster.
It's the why and why not of harsh shadows descending.

Husserlian Meditation: Truck Tires

Ricardo Pau-Llosa

Beside me stalled in traffic, a white pick-up
with four huge worn tires, powdered

in the flour of cement, their treads
a vanquished weave of hexagons

and crosses, ghosts an archeologist
could fathom into spoors, or a chemist

think murk's nascent crystals. I read
erosion, commoner, but I've seen

such blurs mean life, proof, and hope
to other learnings denied me. The lyric

elegist is grateful the light has turned
before he unhaunts, pretending free

in a world vapid grimy. I veer
into the pharmacy lot, and the truck

jolts on, its halo stocks in tow
heaving, galactic, as if awakening.

Mazie Doesn't Know Why

Devon Balwit

Patron saint of bums, every night before turning in,
    Mazie wanders the Bowery,

one step ahead of the Dark Angel, waking the dead
    drunks and dragging them to the closest flophouse.

If they won't get up, she stabs them with her umbrella
    until they rise, Ezekiel's rethreaded skeletons

in the valley of dry bones. She pays the counterman
    for a room, hauling them up and stripping

them to skivvies before tipping them onto thin mattresses.
    In the morning, the same men queue

outside her ticket booth at the all-day theater, hands out
    for a dime to prime the pump with the first beer

of the day. Mazie gives it, ignoring the clucks of the temperance
    ladies, who love neither sin nor sinner.

In lulls, Mazie interprets her dreams, thumbing "Old Gipsy Nan's
    Fortune Teller" or "Madame Futtan's Spiritual Dream Book."

She laughs when they predict dark strangers headed her way,
    the matted hair of sleepers poking over

her movie house seats, suits threadbare, collars greasy, shoes
    down at the heels. When they stagger out,

Mazie makes sure each has enough for a pickled egg, a pig's snout, a
    wash.
    A Jew from Boston, Mazie doesn't know why

she goes to the 2:30 a.m. Night Workers' Mass, why she slips
    a dollar into the poor box or crosses herself

passing stone saints. She'd curse you if you asked,
    but call an ambulance if she stumbled on you

bloodying an alleyway. Mazie sits in the lit glass
    of her ticket booth,

an unlikely niche; The bums feel better knowing
    she's there.

A Blueprint of That Vaster Blue

Paulann Petersen

—*Portland, Oregon*

Within this city built from patterns
intricate as the mapping of stars, I gaze
out my open window and see
two young women—unfamiliar to me—
holding hands as they walk along, leaning
into each other.
                          In a world where ancient cities
mirrored what little we knew of heaven's
own architecture, I hear the two women speak
to an old neighbor lady crossing the street.
They tell her enough of something
about the sweet wiles of false spring
to make the old woman laugh.
Her head held down
by the curve of her spine, she smiles
as she bumps a chrome walker
up and over the curb.
                          From inside this house
deep within a sidereal plan, I watch
the redheaded boys from across the way

chalk basketball plays on squares of sidewalk—
a white-lined map of drives and blocks
for the hoop set at regulation height
above the street outside their house.
Clustered, their X's and looping arrows
emerge like the roughed-in record
of a constellation caught
in motion, a world they people
with cartoon musclemen at war—
slam-dunking, bursting
through a rim.

        May those young women
be lovers, their mouths graced with the salt
of that joy. May they marry
and become a child's two mothers.
May their family of three choose
to live nearby—on the corner,
in that blue house now for sale,
their front garden blooming with starts
of snowdrop, poppy, purple iris
carried to them in welcome by us,
their neighbors.

        May the redheaded boys'
inevitable taunts and shoves give way
to an easy *thonk thonk* of a ball on asphalt.
May their chalk warriors melt
at next rain. The boys, may they play
far into summer evenings—their bodies
crossing through and beyond

the stark boundary of that painted key,

white on dark pavement.

For all comers,

          let them make room.

For Lack of What Is Found There

Andrea Hollander

> *It is difficult / to get the news from poems...*
> —William Carlos Williams

My poems used to hold
wildflowers in them and lichen.
They held the limestone rock
where mosses flourished
and the Ozark woods
where we built our house.

They held a woodpile and a shed
that held a can of gasoline
for my husband's chainsaw.
They held the saw itself,
the shriek of the chainsaw
when my husband cut firewood,
and that odor of fresh-cut oak
and juniper and pine.

Winter after winter my poems
held the warmth of wood
burning in our fireplace.

And when the wood turned to ash
they held the sound of the broom
as I swept the hearth clean.

My poems held the house, too,
and the marriage that thrived
for years inside it, even when
the marriage faltered, even
when it was felled.

No Road

Benjamin McPherson Ficklin

I was the prettiest girl in Cordova and I'm sure that was the only reason Hulky dated me. What I mean is, he didn't care I was smart—that annoyed him. I guess we dated in spite of my intelligence. And the "pretty" comment wasn't as conceited as it sounded. In the winter (the salmon run in the summer) there were only three hundred people who lived in town, so it wasn't like there was much competition.

Constant darkness during the snowy months, but that didn't mean life stopped. To cope with the winters, people either got into hard drugs (shooting heroin or smoking meth) or they read. I usually did the latter. Either way, you needed somebody to fuck and no matter what, you'd end up drinking with everybody else. "The Liver Is Evil It Must Be Punished." Hulky thought that was so clever. He had that phrase printed on fifty t-shirts, figured it out on a stupid website. He sold a few but ended up wearing the rest, a fresh shirt everyday of that winter. "The Liver Is Evil It Must Be Punished." Every day. What a moron. Good riddance, I guess.

Before I get to the end, I need to mention Emmery Sun. I don't know how long she'd been a resident of Cordova. She was older—maybe fifty, but that's hard to say because she worked on the boats and that had a way of weathering anybody. She was definitely *not* from Cordova. People from Cordova have a certain mannerism: defiant in a way that comes off extremely naïve. I'm serious, a lot of those Cordovans never see any other form of civilization. Too afraid of the continual progression that cities supposedly have, they'd rather stay afraid of the wilderness. Scared of the Chugach mountains on one side of their town. Scared of the Prince William Sound on the other. Grizzly bears, tsunamis, a moose is more likely to kill you than a bear, and actually black bears are more likely to kill you than a grizzly. They'll rip out your intestines and eat you while you're still alive. A grizzly will just maul you until you're incapacitated. Anyway, I don't know where Emmery was from. She and I only coexisted in town for one winter and it wasn't like we hung out. But, of course, you knew everybody. There were only three bars and everyone had their favorite. After several hours of drinking, you'd get bored and crawl through the darkness to the bar down on the dock. That's where she drank, so Hulky and I only saw her when we were wasted. We drank on main street. The *point* is that she purchased a gillnetter—a little rusty one-man fishing boat, had somebody haul it past the airport down the gravel road through the muskegs, and set it adrift in the wide brown river that melted off Childs Glacier. She lived there. Even in the winter. I heard that she hunted swans and geese and ducks and fished for anything that would bite.

One of the only things she ever said to me was, "You're misunderstood here. But you know it, that's what makes you great." I think she was talking about my looks. The color of my hair, maybe? I was drunk at the bar on the dock. This was before she moved out to the boat. She told me she hated having to fish, and that she thought it was evil to systematically kill anything. I told her to quit fishing if she wanted and she said it wasn't so easy. She said something about a next step that had to be the right one. I can't remember what I said but that's when she said the thing about me being misunderstood. I never spoke to her again.

Then the bridge that connected Cordova to Highway 10 washed out and we all thought Emmery died. But when the flooding went down, somebody drove out there and she was still living in that old gillnetter, anchored on the upriver-side of what was left of the bridge, protected from the murky rapids full of logs and ice. From then on, our solitude was exasperated. Sorry. I mean the road leading out of town ended in a chained-off jetty. I always thought somebody would get drunk, drive way out there, and fly off the road's end right into the freezing water. At least it offered a good view of the mountains. The last day I was in Alaska I drove out there and stood on that broken bridge for a long time, wondering about the forest on the opposite shore.

Hulky had hunkered down in Cordova before I ended up there (don't ask me how I ended up in Alaska—it doesn't make any sense). Like everybody, he came to make fishing money, but he stayed because that was the one place he could get away with being himself. One time, I remember I was drinking whiskey on his couch and he pulled a bundle of flares out of his little backpack. Everyone has fishing gear up there, so I didn't think much of it, but this stupid grin took his face (like it always did when he was about to act like a little boy) and he walked to the window. Lit a cigarette, lit a flare with the cigarette, yelled something like, "Here we go!" and started hollering as he shot flares across the street at the bar. The orange stains are probably still on the windows. The cops showed up (there were only two cops in town) and they pounded on the apartment's door.

"Hulky, what the fuck are you doing?!" yelled Officer Chuck Brown.

"I'm taking a shower!" Hulky tried hard to stifle his giggling.

"Open the door!"

"I can't hear you! Give me five minutes! Got to finishing washing between my toes!" He sat down next to me, took a pull from the whiskey bottle, loaded a bowl, and we just sat in the flare smoke until the cops gave up. They didn't have a warrant and there was no judge in town to give them one. If they'd arrested Hulky they'd have needed to fly him to Anchorage because there was no jail. As long as you didn't kill anybody or steal anything, you could really do whatever you wanted. So Hulky stayed in that Wild West town because it let him be himself. He was the kinda guy who shot seagulls just because they were flying. I never knew him when he lived back in Olympia, but he told me that he was in and out of jail for disrupting the peace, destruction of property, being drunk and disorderly. The town of Cordova was drunk and disorderly so he fit right in. I only ever found one book on psychology (that's what I tried to get my degree in) at the Cordovan library and I remember it claimed that people need to construct personal narratives to find contentment. That's called living diachronically. The entire town of Cordova (and especially Hulky) was a testament to the inaccuracy of that claim. He and I once got in a big fight about whether or not we were really dating, and all it took was one episode of some sitcom to get him laughing his ass off. I told him he had the attention span of a goldfish. Maybe that's why I was attracted to him, he was always present in the moment. No abstraction at all. He seemed genuinely happy, an exceptional characteristic in such a troubled town. I guess that's rare anywhere.

You could never live in Cordova if you considered your life an ongoing story. You'd leave (like me) or kill yourself. Officer Chuck hung himself, I guess that's what this is all about. I'm not trying to imply it's not a tragedy—it just is what it is. Death is life in Alaska. An average of two fisherman from the Cordovan fleet die every season, lots of overdoses, dead animals show up all over the place (a dead baby moose once floated into the harbor and it rotted there for weeks until some Captain went to tow it past the breakers because it smelt so bad, but the rope pulled right through its bloated stomach).

What I'm trying to get to, and I guess I already alluded to this, is that Hulky was always pissing off the cops. They knew he sold pot, and they hated that, but don't forget it's legal in Alaska. What could they do? But it wasn't just that. There were only three streets in town, so when you're walking to the bars you'd see the big cop car cruising around. Everybody waves at everyone, generally, but Hulky flipped off the cops. I mean, laughing while openly shaking his middle finger at them. Clearly a product of his past conflict with the law, right? Of course, this antagonization resulted in constant harassment.

The morning it all started, Officer Chuck parked right below Hulky's window and blared his siren. This was at 5 a.m. or something. He knew Hulky was hungover. Hulky was so pissed that he got out of bed and started throwing eggs down at the car. Just another morning. Officer Chuck usually got off duty around noon, but that didn't mean he always took off his uniform. Chuck was one of those people who drank at home, but for some reason that day he was getting drunk at the bar on Main Street (everyone has things they're escaping and may- be his was at home that day). Hulky and I went into the bar around 2 p.m. It was already crowded and thick with cigarette smoke. There was probably basketball on TV (it was impossible for me to imagine those games were actually being played somewhere). Billiards was free, so Hulky and I started playing with this Russian guy that everyone called Tod (nobody could pronounce his real name). But Hulky lost the first match, so it was my turn to lose. Hulky went to take a piss and he wasn't gone for more than a second when I heard him burst-out one, loud laugh. A guffaw. He ran out of the bathroom, didn't even glance at me, took his flip-phone from his jacket, kept on giggling and ran back into the bathroom. A minute later he came out and told me we had to leave immediately.

"We're playing a fucking game," said Tod.

"You win." Hulky winked at him, grabbed my purse and ran out of the bar. Outside in the snow and the dark, I started yelling at him. I wanted to play pool. I wasn't ready to walk back to his house. He could barely compose himself enough to say anything, he just kept laughing. He told me that he'd explain everything but that we needed to get back to his house. I wasn't about to take that shit. I probably told him he could go fuck himself and strutted down to the bar on the pier.

The next morning the pictures were everywhere: taped to shop windows, stapled to telephone poles, blowing around in the snow. It was disgusting—Officer Chuck Brown laying on the floor of a bathroom stall (in uniform!) covered in shit and puke, pants around his ankles, empty pint glass in his hand. It really pissed me off. I may not like people, but life's burdensome for all of us. It's better to work on yours than to try and ruin another's. Unless, of course, they deserve it. And that's what Hulky said when I made it up to his apartment. He was trying to instill some pity in me, going on about how he was always harassed by the cops. But whenever a pedestrian trudged by in the snow, he'd stick his head out and holler down at them, laughing like Scrooge on Christmas morning, asking if they'd seen the photos.

I was hungover so we stayed in his apartment, smoking and drinking, fooling around and watching bad TV. It was easy to do nothing when it was dark all day. I was pretty drunk again when the *other* police officer knocked on Hulky's door. Hulky was thrilled, I mean the dumbass was looking forward to this interaction. I can't remember that officer's name, he was a lot younger than Officer Chuck. Hulky answered the door and said something clever but the cop shoved him inside. I could tell something bad was happening because the cop wasn't trying to look like a cop—he looked sincere.

"Chuck's going to kill you."

That was the only time I ever saw Hulky lose confidence. He opened his mouth to say something, grunted, and turned back to me. I hated seeing him like that.

"He wouldn't *actually*, that's ridiculous," I said from where I still sat on the couch.

"I think he really means to do it."

"Where is he now?" I said and finally stood up, lighting a cigarette.

"Getting drunk at the station."

"And what? He said he's going to *kill* Hulky?"

Hulky kept looking back and forth from me and the young officer.

"Yep, exactly. I got to the station this morning and he was already there, in his civvies, holding one of the photos. He was supposed to be on duty, but I was going to let him deal with it. He stayed in there all day. I asked him if he was going to work and he said that he was going to kill Hulky. I didn't believe him, but I've never heard him make a joke before. He asked me to buy him a gallon of vodka, so I did, and now he's getting drunk. I just left the station. He's still holding the photo. The last thing he said to me was, 'I'm going to kill Hulky.'"

You could hear the snow falling and the TV was still playing something. The young officer took my place on the couch and I saw the pistol on his hip. Almost everyone in Alaska owns a gun, most people own a lot of guns, but Hulky didn't. Other than the fishing and the seagull tormenting, there wasn't a violent inclination in him. But he looked *so afraid* in that moment, I could almost imagine him leaning out his window, screaming like a kamikaze pilot, and using the pistol to fire down on sad, old Chuck. The young officer tried to take a hit from my bong but there was nothing in there.

"What am I going to do?" Hulky grabbed my hand, the only time we ever held hands.

"Get out of town." The young cop shook his head and started loading the bowl with the pot in my bag.

"There's no roads!" I hated hearing Hulky sound like that, but he was right. And the ferry didn't leave until the next morning and planes only flew out every few days.

"Do you really think he'd do it?" I asked.

"Yes." The officer inhaled a big hit, held it, coughed but managed to retain the smoke, and exhaled. He stood and said, "I have to get out of here."

"Can't you try and stop him!" Hulky was panicking, which irritated me. Never before had he seemed incapable: Living on a boat for three months, working eighteen-hour days, drinking for the other nine months (drinking more than everybody else could and never seeming that drunk). He was like a tardigrade, and as bizarre looking as one too. I was never especially attracted to him. I think my hope was that if I made him need me, I'd always have something understandable in my life. But he didn't need me.

"Fuck that," said the cop, and he left.

Hulky ran to his room and I thought he was going to crawl beneath his bed or something, but he was done panicking. He loaded the duffle bag he used while fishing: socks, tighty whities, gloves, rope, matches, and all those "The Liver Is Evil It Must Be Punished" t-shirts.

"Are you just going to hide in the woods?"

He scoffed. "No way. He'd find me. I'm going to get to the other side of 38 mile." On the road that led out of town each mile marker was a reference point. 38 mile, like I said, was the bridge.

"You'll die if you swim across."

"If Emmery still lives out there she'll help me." He'd never even said her name to me before.

"And what'll you do on the other side?"

His eyes dulled over in that stupid way. He hadn't thought of that. I imagined him plodding through the darkness and the snow, cursing his fat ass as his toes hardened into purple-blue nubs.

"You'll need snowshoes," I added.

"I love you," he said and squeezed my hand. Really, I believe he meant it. But I didn't love him. I found that out when I hated his weakness so much. I even hated him saying *I love you*. So I just kissed him. I started to feel calm for some reason. Vaguely thankful that I had a reason to leave Cordova. Even in his arms I began severing myself from him. We drove down that terrible gravel road. Maybe there'd been a lot of snow. I can't remember what time of day it was, it could have been midnight or noon; time dissolved into the darkness. We didn't talk and he kept watching for headlights behind us while I kept losing traction on the ice. Forests and muskegs on either side of the road. Wilderness in Alaska always feels like it's watching you. It's aggressively pushing itself on anything human. Maybe that's true for all wilderness, I dunno.

As we approached 38 mile, the trees disappeared and the cliffs sunk into plains of white sand revealing imminent glaciated mountains. All the sand dunes were impermanent, terrestrial acres suddenly disintegrating into the roaring snow melt. The stars and moon reflected brightly off the glacier and cast a yellow hue on the severed bridge. The boat was close to shore. Emmery had adorned it with antlers from game she'd killed. Several dead ducks hung on a line that ran from the cabin to the bow. I parked and Hulky started yelling for her.

A light flickered on in the cabin and it looked like a bear emerged. Emmery was covered in fur, pelts from everything that contributed to her self-reliance. Even her hat was rounded with fur, probably an otter. It was illegal to kill otters, but who was going to report her out there? When there's no one around to enforce laws, it's all just survival and death.

"I need help! Come pick me up!"

"Hulky?" She said it like they had been good friends, accomplices in something, it's possible they had worked on a crew together, but maybe they'd just understood one another from afar. Some people are lucky that way.

"Somebody's going to kill me! Help me cross!"

"That side is too shallow." Her voice was low and it didn't sound like she was shouting (while Hulky was clearly screaming). "You'll have to swim."

"Swim!"

"Swim," she said.

Hulky didn't look at me. He stripped down naked, put his dumb shirt and jacket and pants and shoes into the duffle bag, and stepped into the water—his whole body tensed, sucking in his beer tummy. All he ever wanted in life was to drink and play pool and fuck, but he didn't even hesitate. When he was chest deep and still holding up his duffle bag, he looked at me and said, "It's so fucking cold." He sorta belly-flopped in and swam the rest of the way pulling his bag. Five minutes after he reached the boat they weighed anchor and took off for the opposite shore. I could see the old gillnetter clearly until it drew within the shadow of the mountains. The boat never returned. I tried sleeping in my car but it was too cold. I was worried I'd get snowed in and die.

A week later Officer Chuck was dead, Emmery was gone, and we'd completed an unsuccessful search-and-rescue on the opposite bank. Summer and its daylight was approaching. If he had survived the first month, he was fine as long as he didn't get eaten by a bear. I could imagine him laughing (maybe with her) that stupid laugh at the thrill he'd feel at the first little bit of warmth. I gave up and moved to Las Vegas where I heard you can get paid a lot as a bartender.

There is No Such Thing as Trespass

John Sibley Williams

Having bolt-cutted our way through
the steel mesh separating our world
from the neighbor's slightly larger
share of things, we realize nothing
here is worth stealing we do not
already own. A century compacted
into a single red silo: ours. & inside,
a mountain of uneaten grain. Ours:
three old shovels heavy with earth's
rust propping up a house that in turn
holds up one small corner of a sky.
This rain we mistake for the sky
grieving. Wet, white, bodiless dress
someone else's sister left too long
on a thin line between almond trees.
& ghosts, as always, all around us.
Our dead. Our grief. Our mother's
voice calling us home through holes
built into the fence. & this hurt: still
ours. Same empty place at our table.

Same hunger we mistake for god.
Same cross-stitch of smoke & ash
working its way up the horizon.

Brink of a New Year

Mercedes Lawry

I'm out of breath, watching a scrawl of crows mob
a swooping gull. I cower at the window as if glass
creates a pause between my fretful self
and the maw of the bloated world.
In the long December of a cratered year,
we're left scrambling, alert to the minus tide.
It's the dismissal of truth that storms
our synapses, shifts the pebbled ground,
as if gravity itself has been sucked up
into the clouds. The moon
is no more comfort, the alpine forest emptied
of refuge, the tilt of the earth gone
to a further degree, now perilous.

Mt. Washington in Winter

James Deahl

—for Norma West Linder

State Route 16, old U.S. number 2,
and the Appalachian Trail
all converge in the village of Gorham.
I've not been here since boyhood
when my family's Ford
made it up the dusty auto road,
my father at the wheel.
That, of course, was summer.
Today I arrive with my new wife,
and all 6,288 feet lie under
thick snow; there are few tourists.

George Washington died at 67,
my present age. He never saw
the nineteenth century, nor did I,
being born at the close of World War II.
But throughout my school days
President Washington kept close watch
over my education from his portrait
above the blackboard.

For several years I enjoyed
staying in the Martha Washington Hotel
at Virginia Beach every summer.
My week on the shore was all
hot afternoons spent reading
in the dense shadows of pitch pines,
swordfish steaks for supper,
driftwood fires under evening stars.
Like much of my youth,
her Hotel no longer exists
except on postcards, but
the peak named for her husband
still dominates the White Mountains
and the trail so many hike.

Clear skies over the Androscoggin River;
treacherous ice underfoot.
I wish Norma and I could watch
the winter moon rise full
above these ghostly mountains,
but it's nearly New Moon time.
We go to bed and celebrate our marriage
as a frozen sliver severs
New England's night.

More Than a Howl

Donald Levering

—for the Water Protectors

My friend Peter hauls freight
from Winnipeg to Bismarck, Sioux Falls
to Spokane, Standing Rock to Wounded Knee,
never stopping long enough to fully unload
his cargo of Ghost Dance shirts and peyote.

Now he gets the word to halt his roving
and make noise for water-under-the-ground.
I hand him two harmonicas
and he chews them like camas root,
then trills a few bars of slow blues.

For the first time since I've known him,
Peter grows still, his eyes close.

I study his arroyoed face,
both male and female gathering force
for more than a howl
at those who would wound water,
those who'd nose about ancestor bones

and dig under the river
to lay pipe for pumped crude.

Peter opens his mouth
and a throb begins in bedrock
like an approaching locomotive,
then comes thunder of tons
of snowmelt falling onto boulders,
torrents breaking over river banks,
upending trees, knocking down
poles and walls, flooding streets,

slowing to refill the Missouri's sloughs
and trickle through schist and limestone
into the vast, echoing aquifer.

Broad River

Lex Runciman

Where the Clearances pushed them
To heather, salt water, the rock and wrack
Of Loch Duich, they built houses of stacked stone,
And the narrow rows of seaweed,
That cold slick mess by their hands
Dredged and arranged to decompose,
Those rows have been called lazybeds.

No dark houses, no Clearances here,
Though in Lake County, Glass Buttes
Make an obsidian snow of flakes,
Gray to black, the ancient shard and cast-offs,
Of blade making, scraper, arrowhead, spear—
Patient labor no lies, disease, massacre,
Or treaty or policy could finally silence.

And that white Anglo complicity
Comes to me. With canyons, caves,
Desert washes, playas, painted hills.
With alders, fir, hemlock and cedar.

Columnar basalt by great waters gouged
And cold creeks scoured. North slopes
Snow greened all the way to August.

Easy cut, quick blood,
The slick and dazzle of glass.

Angelina and Joan

Daniel M. Jaffe

Stretching beneath the gold, quilted comforter, Joan asks, "Want me to call Housekeeping?"

"So they can charge $500 for a goddamn new coffee pot?" Out of the bathroom now in just his pale blue boxers, Bob holds up the glass pot filled with water.

"Don't be silly. Twenty-five dollars. Fifty, tops." Joan likes the way the elastic accentuates his pale and freckled love handles. She knows they frustrate him, but they strike her as softly masculine. A whole day and night in luxurious La Jolla, then down to San Diego—how many years since they'd last visited? Two days poking around Balboa Park museums (they skipped the Zoo), then the Midway Museum. Bob even bought her a rose while they strolled through Seaport Village. Two fabulous seafood dinners in the Gaslamp District. And last night, after returning from a couple's Swedish massage in the hotel spa, Bob cuddled her to himself with a tenderness he hadn't shown in…a long time.

Joan folds the gold comforter aside, props her yoga-tight self on three goose-down pillows, makes certain her Victoria's Secret black satin-and-lace babydoll strap slips just enough off her shoulder to entice without declaring obvious intention. So that the initiative can appear to be his.

"The damn thing just slipped out of my hands in the sink and the spout broke off. If you angle it just right, it shouldn't spill." Bob starts pouring water from the broken pot into the black Mr. Coffee machine on the black plastic tray on the antique wooden, bow-legged dresser. Water dribbles onto the dresser. "Shit."

Joan fingers the sideburns of her silver blonde Pixie cut. Too short this time?

Bob lumbers to the bathroom, returns with a hand towel, sops up the spill. "Now they'll probably charge for ruining the polish. Or for a whole goddamn new dresser."

Joan looks out the glass sliding door at their terrace, at the sailboats and yachts beyond. "So pretty, the morning sunlight poking over the marina. Romantic, don't you think?"

"Yeah, sure." Bob tears open a packet of Coffee Mate, pours half into each black mug.

At the border crossing, Angelina shows her worker's visa to Sam, the chubby U.S. inspector she's seen every weekday morning for nearly three months now. He checks the paper yet again and holds out his palm in the universal gesture for "bribe."

Angelina nods, opens the small waxed-paper bag she buys for two pesos before sunrise at her bus stop in the plaza, hands him one of the finger-sized, sugar-coated *churros*. Sam takes it, munches. "*Gracias, mamita.*" His gringo accent always amuses her. "*Hasta mañana por la mañana.*"

Angelina watches her pink net bag (uniform, shoes, hairbrush, trolley pass, churro packet, wrapped lunch tortillas) move along yet another x-ray conveyor belt, then picks it up, steps outside and waits among the familiar commuter faces for the trolley that runs back and forth all day between San Ysidro/Tijuana and San Diego. After shifting her thick black braid over her shoulder, she slowly nibbles the remaining *churro*. With what she earns in her new job, she could well afford to eat a more substantial breakfast. But she's saving because she's got plans.

The trolley arrives and Angelina boards with the crowd. Good fortune—she finds a seat. With thumb and forefinger, she lifts the silver cross hanging from around her neck, kisses it. How comfortable, the red plastic seat.

Seated on the bed cross-legged, now wearing one of the hotel's complimentary white waffle cloth robes, Joan folds Bob's laundry into his suitcase while he, in the bathroom, washes the broken coffee pot and two black mugs. Out of the bathroom, he slips the dried pot into place on the Mr. Coffee burner, positions it so the plastic handle faces front and the broken spout hides from view. He sets the two dried black mugs mouth-down on the black plastic tray beside Mr. Coffee. "There!" he declares, triumphant. "The maid won't have to clean the pot, so she won't know we ever used the damn thing."

"But when she sees the coffee wrapper in the trash—" Joan chooses to keep the pique out of her voice because it's a long drive home—"won't she know we used the machine?"

"Good point. I'll stick the wrapper in my shoulder bag."

"And the used coffee grounds?"

"I'll wrap them up in the wrapper."

"She won't notice they're missing?"

"She'll think we took the coffee packet as a souvenir. The way we're taking the extra soaps and shampoos."

"An awful lot of effort to avoid reimbursing the hotel for a cheap coffee pot that you—that we actually did break."

"It's not like I broke it on purpose. If it'd been better quality, it wouldn't have broken in the first place. Their fault for being so cheap. Any more objections, counselor?"

Joan pastes on a smile. Although Bob loves their infrequent getaways, he resents that her lawyer's income pays for them. Sure, his community college salary covers half their mortgage and other basics, but not their luxuries. Whenever she gushes over his newest article about torture motifs in medieval French theater, he responds, "Your pride and a coupla bucks'll get me a latte at Starbucks. Just not a *venti*."

Bob stands back from the dresser, eyes Mr. Coffee the way a connoisseur might examine a cubist painting. "The next guests might not even use the machine at all. It could be weeks before the hotel discovers it's broken. No way they'll be able to pin it on us."

Angelina looks out the trolley window. So pretty, all those trailers in rows along the trolley line. Between thumb and forefinger, she holds the silver cross hanging from her neck, whispers a prayer to *la Virgen*, who would never permit anything bad to happen to Paco. If only he hadn't gone drinking with those *borrachos* that one time. If only he hadn't gotten himself thrown in jail, a police record.

"There's more than one way to earn American money," he told her after his U.S. visa application came back denied. She begged him not to take her savings to pay the *coyote*, but he was her husband. "It's an investment," he insisted. "I'll send back enough to cover everything in a month. At most, two."

Angelina's eyes burn, her left shoulder aches. If only to sleep just a half hour more. But she mustn't nap on the trolley. If she were to miss her stop and show up late at the hotel, she might lose this new job. Then she'd have to beg for her waitress job back at Sanborns on

Avenida Revolución. Not a bad job, but it paid much less than her new San Diego one.

More to the point: she didn't wish to show her face back at Sanborns. On her last day, after having given notice to her boss, Angelina snuck a croissant from one table's breakfast basket without paying for it. Instead, she billed the customers, a gaggle of *gueros*; blond white men in sports jackets who sat for hours every morning sipping coffee, reading the newspaper, arguing politics, eating half the sweet breads from that straw basket. They would never notice one more croissant on the bill, right?

Even as she shut her eyes in the broom closet to savor the first-time flakiness on her tongue, Angelina demanded from herself an explanation for such theft. How could she? On the way home that day, after cringing at her now-ex-boss's warm congratulations on forthcoming new opportunities *"en el norte,"* she actually stopped by the side of the dirt road and vomited. Hadn't those *gueros* always been polite to her despite her dark complexion, her heavy eyelids? Why had she stolen? And if for some unfathomable reason she had to steal at all, then why from them rather than from someone like the pale young *puta* with her short leather skirts and low-cut red sweaters and gold hoop earrings, always snapping her fingers for Angelina to sweep up the clumps of scrambled eggs the *puta* had dropped onto the tile floor, probably with intention. So cumbersome having to sweep while wearing Angelina's waitress uniform, a floor-length white dress with blue and pink vertical stripes and bright orange triangular yoke, a costume that made her look like some children's cartoon version of Angelina's ancestors.

Angelina resumed saving in the hopes of one day applying to immigrate—legally—to the U.S. Maybe if she earns a good record on her worker's visa? Then she can send Paco back to Tijuana from whichever undocumented job in Los Angeles he has found. Then she can invite him to join her in the U.S. the official way, so he can come legally—the authorities wouldn't be so mean as to let one drunken stay in jail prevent a husband from joining his legally working wife, right? Then they'll live without worry and earn enough eventually to bring her widowed sister over, too. The first day everyone's together in Los Angeles, they'll celebrate in a restaurant. Angelina will pay.

Most important—maybe once a proper foundation has been laid, *la Virgen* will bless Angelina with a child. Angelina confessed her croissant theft to old Padre Jorge who, after reacting with surprise, gave her penance and absolved her. But, are ten *Ave Maria's* truly sufficient?

Five weeks and no word yet from Paco. She worries about the desert. She has heard of *coyotes* abandoning people in trucks to die. Between thumb and forefinger, she caresses the silver cross hanging from her neck, brings it to her lips, kisses it, murmurs.

The trolley stops at the 12th and Imperial Transfer Station, Angelina steps out, waits for the trolley that will take her to the hotel.

Driving up Route 5, just past the La Jolla Parkway exit, Joan notices the highway meridian, a concrete barrier topped with a high black metal fence. Mile after mile. "I didn't notice this fence on the drive down," she says. Then she spots a yellow traffic sign to the right of the road, whispers, "My God."

"Jeez," says Bob.

The yellow traffic sign depicting black silhouettes of a fleeing man, woman, and child reminds Joan of L.A. signs she's seen bearing black silhouettes to caution drivers of road-crossing deer. Bob and

Joan look from the fence on their left to the arid hills and canyons on their right. "Where would they run to?" asks Joan.

"Or from?" asks Bob.

Silence on the drive as she thinks of the mother and small child silhouetted on that sign. As she thinks of her twin, eight-year-old boys.

"I hope the boys had fun at your brother's," says Bob.

She knows he's trying to lighten the mood, so she rallies. "Venice Beach, ice cream, the Santa Monica pier, ice cream, the ferris wheel, ice cream—what's not to love?"

Silence for another hour.

Traffic slows in all lanes. "What the—?" says Bob. They look ahead to see an overhead marquee-like sign flashing: "ALL TRAFFIC MUST STOP."

Joan spots ICE insignia on white mini-vans. "Border control," she whispers.

"We're nearly two hours north of the border," says Bob. "What could they—?"

"If you were illegal, would you stay in relatively small San Diego close to the border? Where someone might recognize you? Or would you head a couple hours north to lose yourself in humongous L.A.?"

All cars slow until Bob and Joan see red stop signs on poles set up between each of the five northbound lanes. An officer in a forest green uniform stands beside each sign and waves stopped cars through, one at a time.

"You didn't slip anyone into our trunk when I wasn't looking, did you?" asks Bob.

She appreciates Bob's effort, but she just can't bring herself to smile.

An officer glares through their Lexus' windshield, makes eye contact with each of them, points a rigid finger—a chill runs down Joan's spine—then waves them through.

Joan feels thankful for her silver-blonde hair, and also feels a twinge of shame. Bob quickly speeds back up to 70.

Angelina pushes her housekeeping cart to the first room of the day and enters. Not much of a mess, thank goodness. She scans for a tip—antique dresser, desk, night tables, bathroom counter. Nothing. Half the time she gets two-three dollars, half the time nothing. The other maids, those with more experience, cautioned her not to take seriously the redheaded boss's pitch that they were paid a low salary because they'd get good tips. "If we don't clean the room well, we get fired. If we do a thorough job, then we're invisible to the guests. Who leaves money for an invisible spirit?"

At least Angelina doesn't have to rent her uniform, she just has to keep it clean. Navy blue with brass buttons and a white collar. A proper dress for a woman, respectable. She fingers the fabric—softer than the coarse gray skirt and blouse she wears on the way to and from work.

Does Paco get to wear a uniform doing whatever work he's doing? He said it could take a while before he'd be able to call or find someone to relay a message. Certainly a couple months before he'd be able to send money. Angelina has much greater patience for money than for news of him. She lifts and kisses her silver cross.

She takes a moment to look out the sliding glass doors at the terrace and marina, a fantasy of private boats. How could so many people afford boats just for fun? Or fancy hotel rooms, for that matter?

She replaces sheets and towels. As usual, she stocks new soaps and shampoos—Gringos are always stealing them. But then—who is Angelina to judge?

Coffee packets are gone, but the mugs and coffee pot haven't been used, so she can save a few minutes by not washing them. A few minutes less in this room and then a few minutes less in others and if she takes no more than five minutes for lunch, she can finish and leave before rush hour and have a chance of finding seats on the two trolleys and bus.

A quick vacuuming of the wall-to-wall carpeting. That's what Angelina wants in her Los Angeles apartment one day—wall-to-wall carpeting soft underfoot. She looks around the room—surely it will pass a spot inspection if her boss checks up on Angelina, as she does at least three times a week.

Joan shuts the stainless-steel refrigerator. "Let's extend the vacation through tonight, okay, everybody, and spare me some cooking? Which'll it be: the Thai place or the ramen place?"

"Ramen!" chime the boys simultaneously.

"Have we got time for a swim before dinner?" asks Bob.

"Sure, Bob," says Joan, weighing how to respond—she wants a pleasant reunion for the boys, after all. "You and the boys go out back for a swim and extend your vacation. That'll give me time to do all the unpacking. Maybe I'll even have time to put in a load of laundry."

He sidles up, reaches around her waist from behind. "Do I detect a hint of sarcasm?"

"Not a hint, Bob," she says, patting his hands at her waist before unclasping them.

"But señora, I didn't." Between thumb and forefinger, Angelina presses the silver cross hanging from her neck.

"This coffee pot didn't just break itself."

If only the redheaded gringa didn't speak Spanish so well, Angelina might claim some language misunderstanding. "Señora, I was in this room not two hours ago. The coffee pot was not broken."

"Just look at it. You admit it was clean and that the guests hadn't used it, so it couldn't be their fault."

"Maybe prior guests?"

"If you'd been honest with me, I'd simply have taken it out of your pay. But you tried to hide it, Angelina. That's what hurts. And now you're lying."

Angelina's face shifts from textured clay to blank stone. "I never lie, señora." No, you don't lie, whispers a voice deep in her head, but...

"You know you were hired on three months' probation. I'm sorry to see you go, but I can't trust you anymore. You can finish the day for full pay, then leave the uniform in your locker. We'll mail your final paycheck."

After her boss departs that first room of the day, Angelina sits down on the bed corner.

She looks out at the marina and boats. She'll miss the daily view.

Angelina shuts her eyes, squeezes them tight, shakes her head, shudders, breathes in deeply through her nose.

Maybe when she reaches home today, there'll be good news from Paco.

Tomorrow, she'll set off early to seek out her old boss at Sanborns—he won't have forgotten her in less than three months. Assuming nobody complained about the croissant, he'll surely re-hire her. Unless he's already replaced her. Which he probably has. But maybe the new girl hasn't been working out so well? Not that Angelina wish-es anyone ill. Maybe business has picked up, and he'll need an extra waitress. Yes, there's certainly a chance. And one morning, when those *gueros* are absorbed in their newspapers, Angelina will slip the price of a croissant surreptitiously into one of the men's sports jacket pockets. No—the price of two croissants.

She fingers her silver cross, lifts it toward her lips, but stops. She sets the cross—unkissed—gently back onto her chest.

She stands, smooths the skirt of this uniform she will miss, moves on to clean the day's remaining rooms.

A Fleeting Haven

Sabrina Stout

Crawling through the tunnels on my stomach
I didn't think about the sea that sucked itself back,
recoiling for the punch. I didn't think
about the abrupt silence of my escape once the door
closed behind me.
Keeping the water out. Keeping me in.
I didn't think about my friends—whether they
dove for the confines of these white walls
or whether the shards of glass
and debris cut their escape short.
I crawled forward, amazed
at how these silken walls kept alight.
     The walls convert your CO_2 back into oxygen
the engineer of this escape route told me
     and the molecules trap light, so your path will never dim.
I didn't ask how. I am not a scientist.
I'm not even sure I'm human. I'm a mouse,
a rat scuttling through pipes below the city.
Thinking of nothing
except my own safety.

Letter from Dragoman, Bulgaria

Jeffrey Alfier

I head out on foot, just as the dark
leaves town and the first streets
awaken, the winding boulevards
uncover with each step a fresh sight:
a woman shading her eyes
against winter's morning sun
climbing its lazy way
over the Tsarichina hills,
the scent of roses and chestnuts
sold by Gypsies,
or the stranger, waking on the overnight
train from Sofia. The way she draws
the curtains to return my stare,
as heavy trucks from Sevastopol
trundle behind my back.
The gaining light scatters
around me. Like the guard tower's spotlight
at Chernevo prison I was released
from in '89—the year the world fell,
sun gaining in amplitude,
warming me like the beggar

who turns his face to the light
in the doorway of a rusted railcar.

Il Principe Ignoto

Turandot

Ricardo Pau-Llosa

What better way to become known by all
than to stay nameless? 'Son of Heaven,
I ask to undergo the trial.' Seems odd no one
inquired if the bold suitor was royal material.

In refugee garb, no guards or entourage.
Persistent, yes, and that heroic fire
the tough princess would mistake for desire
in the gongs of his eyes. But 'she is a mirage,'

her ministers claim, 'the head of a woman with a crown.
A hundred others await, and jewels to boot.'
She is not the prize he is aiming at.
She will be the consort to his renown.

Yet he too must feel dismissed by the past,
strangers forsaking bitterness at long last.

Premonition

Andrea Hollander

Dusk, and the trees barely visible
on either side of the two-lane,
west through the Rockies
in my second-hand Rambler
that growled through the landscape
like some hulking animal.

Our first trip together,
my husband's attention more on me
than on the darkening road,
our newness a kingdom
of only two.

From the forest edge a deer flashed
toward my side of the car,
almost grazing my window.
I gasped—amazed we hadn't hit it.

It could have been a creature
I'd only imagined.
But wasn't that its jaw
and its blazing eye?

Our Rambler growled on
and I laughed. Not exactly laughter
but that giddy foreign sound
that seems to come
from somewhere else.

Like the *falling* part of falling in love:
you leap onto the road unaware
the lumbering beast
speeding towards you
might kill you.

The Yo-yo Champion of the World

Lawrence F. Farrar

On a summer day in 1969, Roseanne Gilbert, a woman in her late-twenties, and her little boy, Griff, sat on a bench in a seaside park. Although the morning fog had burned away, a squint-inducing silvery haze lingered over the water. Haze notwithstanding, Roseanne stared straight ahead, seemingly unaware of the music from a distant transistor radio wafting her way, seemingly unaware of the trucks rattling by on the road to the piers. Across the park a teen-ager sailed a high-flying Frisbee and, like a canine acrobat, his Sheltie caught and returned it to him.

Outfitted in jeans, a blouse, and sandals, Roseanne had short, untidy brown hair. Pug-nosed and fair-skinned, she seemed utterly unremarkable, except perhaps for the fact she had old eyes in a young face. The sparkle that once existed in those eyes had been eclipsed by hopelessness and resignation.

"I wish *I* had a dog," the boy said. He had on shorts, tennis shoes, and a tee shirt with an animal logo—maybe it was a dog. He delivered his appeal with eyes, big and bland, raised toward his mother from beneath the brim of a too-small ball cap. The cap failed to conceal his longish, mussed hair.

"I know, Griff," Roseanne said. "It would be nice. But we don't have the money to keep a dog." As it was, she'd had to count out the coins from a jar to manage the bus fare.

"I'm hungry," Griff said. "Can we get something from that stand?" Like an airborne invitation addressed specifically to him, the aroma of grilling hot dogs penetrated the malodor off the harbor.

Griff fixed his gaze on a two-wheeled, red cart with a beige canvas top bearing the inscription "Frank's Franks." The vendor, a paunchy, red-faced fellow wearing an apron and a ball cap, waved. Griff waved back. He liked the man's shaggy mustache.

"Just wait until we get home. I'll make you a nice peanut butter sandwich," Roseanne said.

Although she'd lost her job, Roseanne still tried to bring Griff to the park at least once a week, usually on Saturday. The park boasted two or three meandering paths, but not much more. In many places the grass had been worn away and in other places it had been smothered by unintended vegetation. All, save one, of the swings were broken. But monitoring the boats out on the bay and watching people with their pets seemed to make the seven-year-old perk up. And, at least for a while, his happiness offset some of Roseanne's despondency.

Roseanne thought of herself as an ordinary person trying to build a new life. All she wanted was a half-way decent life for herself and Griff. Was that asking too much? It seemed as if it was. Even the most modest progress evaded her. To her way of thinking, life had turned out to be arbitrary, unrelentingly unjust.

Her husband had been killed in Vietnam nearly two years before. The military insurance benefits barely provided enough to get by on. And, now her elderly mother who shared their dilapidated apartment had fallen ill. With what she didn't know; just sick. Roseanne anguished constantly—about her mother, about Griff, about where the rent money would come from? What would she do if they were evicted?

She absent-mindedly manipulated her wedding ring. Worthless? How could that man in the pawn shop have said it was *worthless*? People were cruel.

Preoccupied as she was, Roseanne failed to notice a workman who approached them.

Thirty or so, he was broad-shouldered with a longish face, wearing beat-up jeans and a khaki shirt with the sleeves cut off. He'd secured his boots with broken laces knotted together. He needed a shave and, owing to want of barbering, his gray-blonde hair sprouted in odd directions.

He had a long white canvas bag slung over his shoulder and across his chest. In one hand he carried a stick with a nail protruding from the end.

A shy smile played about his lips, and he spoke hesitantly. Looking at Griff, he said, "I found this on the path. Wondered if it might belong to this little fellow." With his free hand he displayed an orange yo-yo. "It's a Duncan." He uttered the brand name reverentially, as if he were endorsing a fine wine.

Roseanne considered him through narrowed eyes. "No. he doesn't have one," she said, her tone dismissive. "Thanks anyway."

The man started to step away.

"Can you do it?" Griff said.

"Do you mean can I work this yo-yo? Why sure." The man turned and leaned down toward the boy. "Just between you and me, I used to be the yo-yo champion of the world."

Dubious, but intrigued, Griff said, "Do you know any tricks?"

"You bet. When you're the champ you have to know quite a few." He emphasized his assertion with a wink.

Roseanne considered the man's claim as close to ridiculous. Yet, he made her boy smile. And in those days eliciting a smile from Griff qualified as a rare feat.

The man slipped off the bag, made a little bow, and flipped the yo-yo back and forth parallel to the ground several times in quick succession. He concluded his demonstration by looping it over his hand and catching it in his palm. Then he gave the yo-yo to Griff.

"I have to get back to work," he said. "You practice. And if I ever run into you again, I'll show you how to *walk the dog.*"

Regarding the man with a wary eye, Roseanne asked, "Do you have a name?"

"I'm Mike. Mike Ryan."

Roseanne hesitated, then said, "I'm Roseanne. And this is Griff."

"Nice to make your acquaintance," Mike said. "Do you come here often?"

"Fairly often. I come for the fresh air. Griff likes to watch the boats. He thinks his daddy might be on one."

"Oh, is he in the Navy?"

"No. He was in the army. Vietnam. He is not with us anymore."

"I'm sorry. I didn't mean to…"

"That's okay. Griff knows, but he likes to pretend"

She remained chary of saying too much. Yet, resist as she would, she instinctively thought well of this man.

"Well, like I said, I have to get back to work or the boss will give me the sack." Mike patted the canvas bag. "And it won't be this one."

Roseanne allowed herself a small laugh, something she rarely did. Now her laughter made her feel self-conscious.

"Never thought back in Nebraska I'd end up this way. But, gotta eat. Trash picker-upper. That's me," Mike said. He offered up a *that's just the way life is* smile.

He made light of it, but she could tell his work embarrassed him.

"Thanks for the yo-yo," Roseanne said.

They surveilled Mike as he moved on down the path, spearing evasive scraps of paper as he went. He delivered each thrust of his clean-up implement with a certain panache, no doubt for their benefit.

Roseanne realized that, like herself, he struggled just to make a bare-bones living.

"I liked him," Griff said.

Me, too, Roseanne thought.

"Do you think he really was a champion?" Griff said.

"Maybe," his mother replied. "Maybe."

The next time they went to the park, Griff hopped into his shorts and slipped on his shirt without prompting. He had the yo-yo in his pocket.

"Do you think we'll see the yo-yo champ?" he said.

"Could be." Roseanne didn't want to generate false hopes. There had already been too many disappointments during Griff's brief time on earth.

So, after they'd been at the park for fifteen minutes, it pleased her to spot Mike marching toward them along the path. This time, however, he toted no bag and wielded no stick.

"Hi," he said. "I kind of thought you might be here today. I liked meeting you the other day. I just wanted to say hello. I hope you don't think I'm out of line or anything."

"I'm sure Griff is happy to see you," Roseanne said.

"Well, I'm happy to see him, too."

Roseanne searched for something to say.

"The bus was awfully crowded today. We could hardly move. It seems like life just keeps piling in on us."

"I know how you feel. Since I got back from the navy, I've been going up and down the coast for a pretty long time. Everything seems jumbled up. It's hard to know what to do."

"Good to hear I'm not the only one who feels life is messed up," Roseanne said. "Things can be pretty rough. It's nice to talk to somebody who can understand." If he only knew how rough, she thought.

"Yeah. I don't get to talk to people much either. That place I stay—it's a kind of boarding house—fellas there are most of them old drunks and none of them too friendly."

For a time, a silence came between them.

"At least we've got warm weather," Roseanne said.

"Yeah. That's something."

Griff said nothing but inexpertly reeled the yo-yo up and down, up and down.

"That looks good," Mike said. "Really good."

"Do you really think so?" A gratified grin spread over the boy's face, as if he'd just won a blue ribbon in the school talent show

"Why sure. Now let me give it a try."

Griff and his mother looked on with fascination as Mike performed an array of tricks, that dazzled them both, including *walking the dog* and *cat's cradle.*

"Tell you what, Griff," Mike said. "I think you need a hot dog. How about it?" He nodded toward the hot dog cart."

Griff looked at his mother for permission.

"That's nice of you," she said. "But I don't think Griff is hungry. Are you, Griff?"

"Aw, come on, mom," Mike said. "Never met a boy who couldn't handle a hot dog. Mustard or catsup?"

"Mustard." Griff avoided his mother's reproachful look.

Mike strode over to the vendor's cart, Griff close behind, like an acolyte trailing a new-found master.

Roseanne kept them in sight as Mike counted coins into the vendor's hand.

"I guess I'm a little short," Mike said.

The vendor looked at him with sympathetic awareness. "It's okay. You can get me next time. Your boy has wanted that hot dog for quite a while."

"Well, he's not my…"

While Griff scoffed down his hot dog, Roseanne said, "I guess he really was hungry." She delivered an appreciative smile, but her lip trembled. She had struggled to retain a shred of pride. She didn't want Griff to take hand-outs.

"I lost my job and things haven't been going too good," Roseanne volunteered.

"Well, that makes two of us," Mike said. "I guess the park foreman didn't think I nailed enough of those candy wrappers and cigarette butts. Anyway, they told me adios."

"It just doesn't seem fair. I bet you were a hard worker. I know I was a hard worker. My boss even said so. Still they let me go."

"Hey, things could be worse. You're young and you have a fine boy."

"If it wasn't for Griff, I don't know what I'd do."

"Well, you've gotta look at the bright side. I got some good news I didn't get to tell you. I already got a new job."

"Oh, that's fine."

"It's only as a laborer at that new pier they're building. I was hoping to get on as a longshoreman. But it seems like you have to know somebody. I don't know anybody. Anyway, this will be better than rounding up the trash."

"I'm glad for you, Mike."

"You know, Roseanne, to tell the truth, I've been kind of down. Just scratching out a living, you might say. Sort of gave up on things. Hope you don't think I'm talking out of turn, but seeing how you're holding up and how you treat Griff, you know that kind of sparked me. I can't put it in words very well, but I figure I should have more hope; try to be more like you."

"Well, I don't think I deserve that, but I appreciate you saying it. Good luck in your new job." Downcast as she was, the fact she could inspire another person seemed incredible, but the knowledge lifted her up, at least for a little while.

"I'm not real smart. But I guess I have to keep on trying," Mike said.

"I'll bet you'll do just fine."

She sensed a kind of good-hearted innocence about him.

"I've been thinking. I should never have quit high school. But maybe I can still go to some kind of school. Get a good-paying job; like a welder or an auto mechanic. I'd like to do that."

"Why not? Me, too. We both could do something." She wasn't sure she believed it. But she wanted to believe it.

Once Mike said goodbye and was on his way, Griff said, "Mama, is Mike a good guy?"

"Why do you ask, Griff?"

"Cause you told grandma you wished you could meet a good guy."

"Oh. Well, I think he is a good guy. We'll see."

"Was my dad a good guy?"

"Sure, Griff he was a good guy."

"I like Mike," Griff said.

Roseanne nodded and let slip a little smile that seemed to signal, *we both do.* If she gave Mike hope, she thought, it was a two-way street. He gave her hope, too.

A week later, Roseanne and Griff encountered Mike again. This time, he handed Roseanne a small bouquet of flowers. She realized he'd likely picked them somewhere in the park.

"What kind of flowers are those?" she said.

"I don't know. I just thought they were pretty. Kinda like you. Hope you like red."

She barely knew Mike; yet she felt there was something solid about him, something decent. And, like herself, he was a lonely person, struggling to survive in a difficult world. The flowers gratified her. Until then she'd come to believe hers to be a life left behind.

"They're real nice, Mike. Real nice."

She knew he was drawn to her. And she was drawn to him. But she worried; she could endure no further disappointments.

Mike had something in a paper bag. Griff knew he was not supposed to expect anything. Nonetheless, he fixed his gaze on Mike and on Mike's bag.

"Did you think I forgot you, Griff?"

Humility personified, Griff said nothing. But he remained as expectant as the sparrows fluttering about their feet, ever hopeful some tidbit would find its way to the ground.

Mike reached into the bag and retrieved a kid's baseball glove. "I knew you wanted one."

"I never had a glove," Griff said.

"I hope you don't mind it's second-hand," Mike said, to Roseanne as much as to Griff. I saw it in the Goodwill. I knew Griff was a right-hander, and I figured he just had to have it."

"Thanks, Mike. I'm sure he's going to like it a lot," Roseanne said.

"The lady at the Goodwill was real nice. She even threw in a ball—free. She said it went with the glove."

"Can we try?" Griff said.

"Sure why not? Let's go over there behind the benches. I'll roll you some grounders."

And off they went.

Roseanne watched from a distance. Griff lacked any natural skill; and Mike was not much better. But it didn't matter—not at all. It felt good to watch the two at play. It felt good to hear them laugh and giggle.

On the bus going home Griff said, "I like Mike. He plays with me." Griff clutched the mitt with the ball inside against his chest with two hands.

The following Saturday Roseanne and Griff had been at the park for nearly an hour and there had been no sign of Mike.

"I guess he's not coming," Griff said. Like a ship's lookout, he'd been searching the horizon for Mike almost from the moment they arrived.

"Well, he probably had something to do. Anyway, he never promised he'd come by every time we're here."

Just then, however, Mike came striding down the path. Red-faced and out of breath, he said, "I missed the bus and had to walk. I was hoping you'd still be here."

"It's okay, Mike," Griff said, "I forgot the yo-yo."

"Maybe next time," Mike said. He looked at Roseanne. "I guess I'm presuming a lot; about *next time*, I mean."

"Don't worry. We come to the park anyway, and it's nice to see you."

Mike delved into his pocket. "Here you go, Griff. I got these jelly beans for you. I hope you like jelly beans."

"You don't have to keep giving him stuff," Roseanne said. "But thanks anyway"

"I like jelly beans," Griff said. "Especially these red ones."

"How is the job going?" Roseanne said.

"Going great. Good boss and the other guys have been helpful. They've been teaching me to build forms for concrete."

"That's good. You know, Mike, Griff and I have enjoyed meeting you."

Mike sheepishly examined his boots, but he couldn't hold back a smile.

He cleared his throat and then cleared it again. "Roseanne... Roseanne. Geez. I'm kind of nervous. I get paid next Friday and I was wondering if maybe...if maybe you'd like to go to a movie with me. Maybe a burger afterward."

Roseanne hesitated and then said, "I'd be happy to go with you."

"That's the best news I've had in a long time. An expression of near-rapture crossed Mike's face. "Yes, sir. The best."

"I don't remember the last movie I saw. What's showing?"

"It's about a lion. At the Seaside. It's called *Born Free*. Griff could go, too, if you want."

"He's a little young. Let's just make it the grown-ups."

"Okay." Mike thought for a moment. "Maybe we can go see *True Grit*. It's at the Strand. Do you like John Wayne?"

"Yeah, he's okay. You decide."

"Okay." Mike thought for a moment. "I guess I'm kind of plain to look at. But if I was to put on a necktie, I bet you'd think I was a pretty good-looking dude."

They both laughed.

Roseanne began to hum—and then to sing. *Someday We'll Be Together.*

"You have a pretty voice, damn pretty." Mike said. "I like hearing it."

"Not really. I can't even remember the words. But somehow I just felt like singing."

"One of the guys said I could borrow his car. So I can pick you up at your place. Say, 6:30."

"I'll wait on the corner of Bingham and High. We don't have a phone; so don't forget."

"Don't you worry, Roseanne. I'll probably get there early."

Cautious, she needed to no know more about Mike Ryan. At the same time, Roseanne felt as if she'd chanced upon an oasis of hope on a dark night.

Roseanne put on a blouse and skirt; did what she could with her unruly hair; added some lipstick; and at 6:15 declared herself ready.

"Now, Griff, you be nice to grandma while I'm gone. If she wants a drink of water or anything, you bring it to her. Okay."

Griff nodded. "Can I see Mike?"

"He's picking me up with a car. You can look down from the window. I'll tell him to wave. Okay?"

"Will he see me?"

"Sure. Anyway, I have to go now. I'll see you when I get back."

She gave Griff a hug.

"I'm going, Mom," she called out. "Griff had his dinner."

Her mother answered from behind a bedroom door. "Don't come home too late."

Roseanne made her way down three flights of dimly lit stairs and went out on the street. She looked up and saw Griff stationed at the window. He peered out from behind a tattered curtain.

She should have given Mike her apartment address, but she hadn't wanted him to see how shabby the place was. She wanted to make a good impression.

There was little traffic and, except for two or three people going into "Pay Day Loans" across the street, she saw few pedestrians. Scanning the traffic that did approach, she wondered what kind of car Mike might be driving. Did he even have a license?

She looked up and blew Griff a kiss. He sent one back. If it hadn't been for Griff, she thought, I don't know what I would have done. But now, perhaps...

"Hi, Roseanne." It was old man Anderson hobbling by with his cane. "What brings you out here?"

"Oh, I'm just waiting for someone."

"Anybody special?" He underscored his question with a knowing smile.

"Just someone. Nice seeing you, Mr. Anderson."

As Anderson doddered into the building, Roseanne glanced up. Griff still maintained his vigil at the window.

Roseanne had no watch. But she sensed the minutes ticking away. Screams of distant sirens touched her nerves, stirred feelings of unease.

Where was Mike?

She paced back and forth. He couldn't have had a problem locating the intersection.

Another neighbor passed by. Inquisitive looks but at least no questions.

She waited. And then she waited some more. But Mike did not show up.

In the end, Roseanne gave up and trudged back up the stairs to her apartment.

"I didn't see Mike," Griff said when she came in.

"Neither did I," his mother said. She turned her head so the boy could not see the tears welling up in her eyes.

Griff remained at the window, until Roseanne shooed him off to bed.

A week passed and Roseanne heard nothing. The park no longer held any attraction for her, but Griff begged for one more visit.

"Come on, Mommy. I won't forget my yo-yo this time. I want to show Mike my new trick."

They'd been on the bench for a half hour or so when the vendor maneuvered his cart into its familiar parking space. Griff waved at him.

The man walked over, a somber look on his face, and said, "I'm sorry. It's too bad about your friend."

Roseanne looked at him with a puzzled expression. "What do you mean?"

"The accident."

"What accident?

You mean you didn't know?"

The vendor hurried back to his cart and returned with a newspaper. "It's right here. You can see for yourself."

"We don't get a paper," Roseanne said.

Her eyes fell on the headline. 'One Killed, Two Injured.' "One man died and two were injured as the result of an accident Friday afternoon at the Pier 27 construction site. Scaffolding the men were on collapsed for unknown reasons, plunging them into the bay. One of the workmen, Mike Ryan, 33, landed on a camel (float). Police say he died of a broken neck. The other two men, Charles Gadbois and Ralph Phillips, suffered only minor injuries. The incident is still under investigation."

She crumpled the paper and let it fall to the ground.

"Geez, lady. I'm sorry. I figured you knew. They say it wasn't very high."

Griff looked away and fiddled with his yo-yo.

To no one in particular, Roseanne said, "It was all hot air. Mike didn't know what he was talking about. Life's hopeless; there's nothing. I should have known."

The injustice of it all. The spark of optimism had been snuffed out. What now? she thought. What now? Hopes dashed, the unfortunate widow was once again on her own.

C94

Simon Perchik

The long black coat passing by
covers these headstones the way all riverbeds
are hidden from the ice, give up land

for its warmth—some darkness
would be enough, would reach the ground
before turning back as the shadow

helping you collect—a few small stones
no longer together would fit into one sleeve
more than the other—with such a weapon

these dead slowly disappear into moonlight
where the heat from far off becomes brighter
though it knows how cold you are

that you go to bed wearing a fleece-lined jacket
are following alone, counting backwards
as if you were returning something.

Lives in the Balance:
A Review of Rafael Alvarez's *Basilio Boullosa Stars in the Fountain of Highlandtown*

Sue Mach

"How many sins could you commit in one day and still tell yourself you were a good man?" After skipping a traditional Christmas Eve dinner and screwing up an untraditional one he was supposed to be having with his girlfriend, the character of Wigmann contemplates this question as he downs a liver and onion dinner at a Baltimore harbor-side bar while thumbing through passages of *The Diary of Anne Frank*, deciding whether or not he will go to the pier, upon his mother's request, to pick up a visiting Spaniard from the Old Country. All of the themes of Rafael Alvarez's evocative collection of short stories, *Basilio Boullosa Stars in the Fountain of Highlandtown*, coalesce in this moment. The question of goodness and the search for beauty are underlying currents throughout these stories.

Wigmann is a featured player in the first story, *I Know Why I Was Born*, which begins on the day that our star, Basilio, (age eight) wakes up and realizes he was "[b]orn to paint the pictures in his head, to sketch the kitchen in the basement, to capture the clouds as the wind drove them past the bottle cap factory down by the railroad tracks, to capture the air that swirled across the tarred rooftops." The stories are roughly chronological and follow Basilio from his artistic awakening to his free-fall from a scaffold while painting a mural, "a plunging pint of Hellenic blue about to mix with the thin blood of an 86-year-old artist who'd never received his due."

While Baltimore is his canvas, Basilio's chorography is the soul. The book was published on the twentieth anniversary of Alvarez's first short story collection, *The Fountain of Highlandtown*, and the short story from which the collection bears its name appears in both books. Reading the story a second time in a different context is a unique experience because now we know Basilio as a middle-aged man who, in both his paintings and his life, is simply trying to get things right. Divorced and out of a "real job," he moves from the suburbs to Macon Street to live with his Spanish grandfather. "Why are you here?" the old man asks almost daily. It's a question that never escapes the artist.

Art, for Basilio, is a way to capture the past and still the motion of constant change in which rituals and traditions are turned upside down. For instance, not long after his divorce, Basilio fake-marries a woman in an Elvis bar where they fish their rings from a tank of abandoned wedding bands. The truest moment of the story is when the woman, Roxanne, literally bears her breasts and asks him to paint her.

Basilio's great obsession is his distant cousin, Nieves, "...both kin and stranger, all of nineteen years old," who arrives unannounced from Spain to live with him and his grandfather in an attempt to escape a drug addiction. For Basilio, Nieves brings "[a] sense of being in Spain though he'd never been, a transcendence of time and place he tried to understand but never felt from the stories he'd heard from Grandpop all his life, the stories he'd begun to paint after moving in." Basilio abandons all common sense; instead he tries to discover Nieves by painting and sketching her. In the end, not unlike the genetic memory of a past he will never know, she becomes lost to him—both literally and figuratively, after she's arrested for shooting heroin. She leaves the house and folds into the city. Neither Basilio nor this American Jerusalem can save her.

Alvarez is a kind of urban Proust, favoring pickled pig's feet over madeleines, and baseball stadiums in lieu of French drawing rooms, all underscored by a rock and roll soundtrack. Things fall apart. A sober Basilio arrives too late in the eighth inning of an Orioles game in an attempt to reconcile with his wife. Expressways plow through immigrant neighborhoods. In order to get his daughter access to private Catholic education, Basilio makes a deal with a beer drinking nun to restore paintings in a church and school that will vanish the following year. Still, from the rubble comes some kind of rebirth, and the artists—both Basilio and Alvarez—bear witness. These stories strike a profound balance between motion and stillness, the sacred and the profane—the tension of which achieves the beauty they seek.

Born and raised in Baltimore, Maryland, Rafael Alvarez learned on-the-job-journalism at the Baltimore Sun, *working his way up to City Desk where he befriended all manner of characters: dishwashers and detectives and dancehall queens—all of whom would eventually find their way into his fiction. A writer for the first three seasons of the HBO series* The Wire, *Alvarez published a collection of short stories in 2014,* Tales from the Holy Land. *Some of his other works include:* The Sandman's Pentateuch, Orlo & Leini, Rolling With the Seasons, *and* Hometown Boy. *His short story, "The Road to Hibbing", was featured in the 2015 volume of the* Clackamas Literary Review. Basilio Boullosa Stars in the Fountain of Highlandtown *is published in honor of the twentieth anniversary of his collection of short stories titled* The Fountain of Highlandtown.

Grammar Lesson

Andrea Hollander

The word *lie* is a verb
that's also a noun: He lies,
and his lie multiplies.

But *to lie* also means *to recline*:
She decides to lie down again
on her side of their unmade bed.

To *lay* means to place:
As he speaks, she lays
her coffee cup on the table.

But *lay* is also the past tense of lie:
She lay there the rest of the day,
barely moving.

Laid is the past tense of *lay*:
When he left, he laid his house key
on the counter.

About the colloquial way
we sometimes use *laid*,
need I say anything?

Languuissant

Charles Tarlton

i

*Smother a sphinx in goodwill butter? Cut the lifeline lest
it be an umbilical cord?*

—Robert Duncan

from now forward each is born completely new
light years and a fallen bridge between

these are the people of my grandmother, all dirt farmers, and children
without shoes,
with a handpump on the wooden kitchen sink

*the Hominini tribe (humans, Australopithecines and other extinct bi-
ped genera, and chimpanzee) parted from the Gorillini tribe (gorillas)
between 9 million years ago...*

in lines of change a degree can be so large it feels (O, so it is!) a change
in kind
the changes from that harddirt life in a Missouri village in the 1930s,
to the swish
going by of an electric car

ii

The fineness, and the practice, lie here, at the minimum
and source of speech.

—Charles Olson

as if someone let fall outward down the rilles and runnels a cold rain
gouging the soil, scratching in the mud the names

of beautiful flowers. Do you believe the call of the birds, crows and
    doves

we'd provoke them in the Eucalyptus tops and how they'd fly, cry out
    and around
then settle back like parakeets or butterflies

all the poems in the world there in the aromatic peel of an orange

iii

if they do this they need a catalogue.

—Gertrude Stein

what the land offers
under its morningcoat of broken asphalt
and fantasies

depending on the angles
long or short, whether the rolling surf
flattens or rushes up

in the jungle of Maples and White Ash
at the back of our yard
a nuthatch calls out invisibly

doesn't everyone already realize
the delicious mystery of tire sounds
on pavements in the rain

there's finality as the coming darkness swallows
the light insatiably
encroaching, taking it all

iv

Inanimate in an inert savoir.

—Wallace Stevens

with both the front and back doors open the sound flows through here
    like a little river
and the grind of a car going by is like a tree

broken off and floating in the stream and somewhere out there sounds
    that could be a
wooden mallet against a tree trunk

a barrel rolling up the ramp, or the woman next door sorting through
    her garage
the purr of my refrigerator

fights its way past the crinkle of tinnitus in my ears. There, do you hear
it?

A dog was barking before, but not now

Partial Eclipse

Jennifer Dorner

—Carlton, Oregon: August 21, 2017

Fixed to the moon's slow progress
as it crosses paths with the sun,
my father and I sip coffee
on the patio waiting to watch
the light break down,
each of us trying to move
to the next phase of our lives:
waning into the seventies,
waxing toward starting a family.
We settle on a partial solar eclipse,
off by tenths of a degree.

In the polymer glasses we see
black infinity, a blazing star,
as squirrels race up firs and birds
arrow the feeder, plane after plane
departing overhead. We count
the minutes to maximum eclipse
measuring the distance in shadows
until a frog croaks and a cricket

rubs its wings.
Slope winds stir as temperatures drop,
even in shade, the sun's thinnest crescent
cooling our skin,
twilight in totality's scattered edge
a pale yellow band on the horizon.
Then Venus, morning star,
high in the ashen dusk. We are suspended

in this apogee, the hair on our necks rising
          to the pure quiet, then gunshots
over the field, the corona's halo of secrets
unveiled in the indigo-dark three miles south

and as the pendulum moon swings
through the galaxy we delay
returns to the hardware store and office

for an honest talk full of gratitude
as today restarts the light in the light.

The Lost Coast

Michael J. Shymanski

I select a few flasks of bourbon from the wall and the little woman says, "Along with those beers?" referring to the six in my hand that I forgot I'd snagged and when I nod, she asks if I'm driving the rig gesturing to my Sedan, which is hardly a rig at all. I nod again and she goes, "You been drinking today, son?"

Before I can answer, the door explodes and a man doused in dirt appears straddling light. A dusty aura seeps around him into the store and there is something holy about him, light glowing off the texture, like filth can shine. He is looking at me wet-eyed muddy deltas running and I am looking at him, the twin slivers of pink that cut across his brown caked face like a tender wound and they fissure open, "That you shooting down Wilder Ridge?"

I'm too afraid to speak and sound drunk so I shake my head.

"Don't lie."

He steps forward, dust falling off his body. My hands go up.

"You're a visitor here."

"Ed," said the little woman stepping around the counter. "Come have a seat."

She herds him around to a little stool and pats his shoulder and the dirt springs like fleas and flutters like ashes. Ed, the Holy Man on the stool, is taller than her and she stands beside him, under him, and patting him with her old soft hands whispering cool like his conscience. I try to thank her, ramming words through the concrete lodged in my throat. But she does not hear me, muttering to Ed, "Let them be, let them be. That's why they call it 'boisterous.' Can't spell it without 'boys'..."

On the car—the same color as the frenetic man—Darius and Alvin are looking long into the dirt road that leads to the trailhead. I hand them bottles. I don't tell them I've bought whiskey. The details are hazy but I think Darius opposes and then cedes when I open two for Alvin and myself.

"Where's the gas station?" Darius asks.

"I said fuel, not gas."

When Alvin gets halfway through his, he slips around the building out of sight. I look at the perspiration on his bottle, trickling onto the car. The sound of heaving penetrates the sun-hot silence.

"You really did him in last night," says Darius.

"It was just a few drinks."

Alvin and I started with a few beers at a dive. He bought first and then I put down my credit card because my account numbers haven't been as strong recently but we had not reached the minimum so I had to order another round and close out. Shots came from the house—I'm a regular—and I ordered another to cool our throats and by the time I closed out again Alvin was glowing like a lantern.

"Just hope the guy's alright."

This trip is for Alvin. He is "going through it," according to Darius, because things ended with his girlfriend. Darius and I—mostly Darius—threw this trip together, for Alvin. To get out of the city, for Alvin. To distract or heal or something, for Alvin. *Alvin's* weekend. But I went along with the plan, mostly because I needed to escape the gloom of concrete and high-rises.

Alvin comes back and slips into the car like a child waiting for his mother.

"You okay, buddy?" I ask.

Alvin's as good as dead in the backseat. Swollen eyes. Body depending on the door. His body ripples to a soft burp.

"Hair of the dog," I say to Darius. "Once again, booze for the win."

"That's a terrible attitude."

"Don't be a wet blanket."

I polish off Alvin's beer. My car is the same color as Ed the Holy Man but it lacked the aura of the seething shoulders and its smaller, gentler company. There are two buttprints—my friends'—and then the dark brown ring of where a half-drunk bottle once stood.

I can't remember how exactly we start the hike but I know I get into it with Darius over fire. We sign permits at the self-service station and make donations. Darius spots me because I left my card at the bar last night.

"It says 'No fires under any circumstances,' guys," says Darius. I shake my head and Alvin shows no reception, like he's receiving data by DSL. "Right here, on the placard."

The placard—laminated computer paper—maintains the phrase in capital letters.

"We're having a fire," I say. "I'm not *not* having a fire."

"No, we *can't*," Darius says. He's a rule-follower, a people-pleaser, a do-gooder.

"Says who? Ominous font?" At least they didn't veto alcohol. "What's more terrifying for you? Helvetica? Times New Roman?"

His face says, "Fuck you," but his mouth says my name with some force and a little plea. I'm already on the trail in the dunes. When

I think about it, I know it has nothing to do with fire. Darius is my best friend. Fighting is frivolous. We'd manage. Get over it. Make up. But there's the sturdy career, depth in bank balances, a fiancée. There are men that have everything and Darius is one. I hate him a little for it. I hate him a lot for it. It isn't the fire that's between us.

"You hear about Terry Combs?"

We turn off the dunes to bluffs beneath steep hills. Sparse vehicle traffic imprinted the trail and the two of us are walking side by side in the parallel hollows. Alvin sags behind us, his pace a half-dead lurch.

"Yeah." There is a lighthouse in the distance and I wonder how long it will take to get there and what we will be talking about and I hope it isn't this.

"He just dropped off the continent a couple months back."

"Yeah?" I say, in flimsy innocence. This was a story I know—very well—and a story I do not like.

"Apparently got disillusioned with reality. In public. At a bar."

I trace the trail to my boots.

"But he's back in the Bay Area. Looking for a job. Just out of thin air."

This is news. I knew about Terry Combs and witnessed his trifles, or at least thought I knew. I ask, "Any luck?"

"He just started, so not yet," he says. "Wild, huh?"

I escape into the land, the trail snaking the golden bluffs that tumble into the ocean. We backpack beneath rolling hills freckled with hills, gold and beautiful from seasonal death.

"Heard it was like a light switch. *Click*. Then he lost it," he says. "Could happen to us, I guess."

I look at the lighthouse. The hills, bluffs, beach. I can't hide any-where. I know this story because I was there when he let his marbles run. Janine had just gone and Terry Combs had screwed things up in his sales job, empty-handed for the second month in a row. It could happen to us because it did happen to us. It happened in some dive bar in the Tenderloin or the Mission or Outer Sunset, if I recall right. We met to take the edge off, collaborated to commiserate. We poured enough acid on our problems so the screaming turned to a muted gar-gle. I knew when Terry Combs lost it because I stuck my fingers in his mouth and poured the roiling nectar down his gullet.

And as they say, Terry Combs went *click*.

At certain points we have to run from waves, through wet sand to dry sanctuary. While Alvin hustles surprisingly quick with a pack on, Darius doesn't and the ocean wraps a salty hand around his boot.

"Whose job was it to check the tide chart?"

"No idea, but I'm the booze camel," I say slapping my pack.

He takes a long, knowing look.

"Okay, this one could be my bad." I put a hand on his shoulder. "But last night I got drinks with Alvin, for Alvin."

We kept running, tripping over stones ranging from the size of a heart to the size of a car. We run up a stratified staircase by twos, and while Darius and I scramble out, Alvin's stuck in a rocky hollow. The thunder is portentous. Realizing he's fucked he—in feeble gesture—covers his face with his hands. The break strikes mid-thigh, rocking him, moving past, climbing the walls of the alcove, and encasing him in a foam coffin.

He climbs out slow and wordless, permitting waves to hit him, immune to the prospect of further wetness. Darius gives him a towel and I give him bourbon; warmth on the outside and inside.

"Man, he's getting reamed today," says Darius down the trail. "Hope he's okay."

I tell him to stop saying that kind of shit, his exorbitant sympathy grating against my good will. I know this trip is for Alvin and it's Alvin's weekend but to clarify, Alvin broke up with his girlfriend. Alvin elected tragedy. It did not seek him like it had done me. He'd be fine.

I actually cannot remember if Alvin getting soused happened on this particular trip or another that we took to the Lost Coast but I know that once we continue trekking, the northern winds embrace us. The drink kicks and I spread my arms coursing with the viscous flow of thawing blood. The sun is warm and the wind aides us south and I'm drunk and it's alright. I lost my job in the city and have feeble numbers in my accounts but out here none of that matters. Currency here is the fortitude of my own feet and the will to move. My blood is gasoline burning and none of my organs are sore. The waves lick my lower half and my feet are swimming in my boots. It's alright. I'm alright. I'm wet and sore and stumbling but I feel like everything inside of me at this moment is good.

The landscape had taken a bite out of gutted house and swallowed all but the kitchen, breakfast nook, and front door. Alvin's asleep at the base of the sink in a puddle. I go to the window of the nook and look out to the crescent inlet. I try to imagine a pair of lovers looking out, unaware of the rampant surroundings looking in. I pour some beer— the last beer—out on the warped floorboards because it seems like the right thing to do.

Darius lies out on the porch. I step over him and walk around the building because I want to be alone. I crawl inside a bathtub in the backyard, finish the beer, and pull out a flask of whiskey.

I try not to think of her so I think of the coast. I think of everything—houses, engines, roads, lighthouses, people—that had been abandoned and then claimed in the territory war between the oceans and hills. I think of the grass that tickles our shins. I try not to think of the way she died, dangerous thoughts, unbridled like the landscape, thoughts that could send someone to ruin, a hundred precise moments strike me like a bad mosaic of sobriety. I close my eyes. The briny grain caresses me in the wind. I try to move from what was to what is, to here and now, to the bathtub, hills, bluffs, beach, the trail, but end up at what could be. Instead of bottle and ocean and rust she's here, here in the tub, between my legs, her back on my stomach and head shelved on my collarbone. I try to wrap my arms around her. There's a welling, a shackled something rising in my stomach, scraping ribs, unfolding ugly wings. I pour bourbon in my mouth but my throat chokes and I cannot swallow. I pour half the flask in my mouth before my sinuses burn, my throat gives, and hot bashful tears explode from the sockets.

"You can't be drinking here." A dilapidated window frames a woman beside a littler human. The shingles had fallen off the façade. I imagine the wilderness ripping them off tenderly like an interrogator would do to fingernails.

"Wind's got me crying," I say. I rub the tears into my cheeks. The woman's got on the fat chunky glasses people wear over prescription lenses. Also, a bucket hat. The littler human wears the same thing in the same hue—backpacker olive—and I'm willing to bet they have those cargo pants that zip off to dweebier cargo shorts. The littler human is young. I put my chips on him being a boy. "How old is your son?"

"He's not my son."

The boy is silent. He's a badass for suffering the trek. Or a dork. Betting the latter. I stand in the tub, hands on my hips, mildly aware how ludicrous I seem.

"How old are you?"

"Don't talk to him, swine."

I laugh. I like these people. I ask again, she hurls a diluted insult. Apart from insults and poor disposition, they're enjoyable, enjoyable geeks with a profound lack of social skills, sure, but they're keeping me here. I ask if they saw a laminated placard about the dress code and I black out. When I black in, I'm laughing some point down the trail, forcing myself to think of the quip, laughing so hard I'm crying knowing it's easier the second time around and the cap, the cap to the whiskey is gone, stolen by the land, so I decide to drink the last shots as I move on.

To his dismay, I light a fire.

We forage on the bluffs for tinder and throw the dead grass on the flames by the armful, igniting on contact, forcing us to retreat. We dance like this for a while, collecting, stoking, the burning and blackening of tinder and kindling, our two steps back, one forward. Eventually the coals stabilize on the desolate beach, bathing the cliffs as fire diminishes on the horizon. Darius sits on a log of driftwood, arms crossed, not daring complicity. He scowls into the fire half angry, half entranced. Alvin has come around, the shock therapy of the salt bath dredging out his spirits, swapping pulls with me, taking the flask instead of me giving.

I stand up too fast—the "wobbles," we call it—leaving blood in my feet and sobriety in the sand. Sometimes drunk sidles up to you and submerges you, baptizing you delirious. I go after the waves like a child, chasing and retreating and yipping and giggling. Alvin joins. I remember being without a shirt at one point but not taking it off. My backpack explodes on the beach, clothes everywhere, and I dig for the final flask. I burrow my feet in the sand. I take the flask from Darius not remembering he came along. I'm rubbing his bald black head and begging him to not get married. The fire rages taller than me. I turn around and now it's dark and the tide is low and the cold air lacerates my skin. Alvin throws his arm around me. I cannot remember what he says, if he says anything. I turn around and a man—a stranger—coils his face.

"What are you doing?" I say.

"No," says the man. "What are *you* doing?"

A badge flops out and catches firelight. Alvin groans. I think I call him Ranger Rick or Deputy Dingleberry. Of all things going on, Darius is mad at me. The next thing I remember is whipping it out and pissing on the flames and yelling slander. I couldn't see the ranger or my friends because after peering into the fire for such a time the rest of the world turned so dark.

I'm sobering dangerously when I slip into my sleeping bag beside the car. Darius and Alvin are breathing softly in sleep but I cannot find the solace myself, limbs howling after a blurry hike. I roll and fight with my sleeping bag until I end up on my back, still as the night, insides boiling.

I seek refuge in the stars. The absence of light pollution baits the more timid ones to play and I can lose myself in the overwhelming vastness of the sky. Stars have color here: red giants, blue giants, and the more familiar ones like the sun. Shooting stars slash the sky open and satellites cruise on a languid drift. I know profoundness resides between the lights and I stare long into the dark. I go seeking something, some cosmic thing I had never seen before, something I cannot describe to lift me out. The stars come down like stalactites and pin me like Christ. In the abyss the city looks back at me, the cradle, everything. Zeros bounce around in account balances. The weight of the sky bears on me. My kidneys and liver fight like rabid dogs. The stigmata forces my eyes open, long days and short nights at bars on rerun. The black mass presses and deflates my lungs. I see the topography that turned against me, every hill and valley reminding me of a rise or gulley in her body. I moan but no sound exits my mouth. The sky grinds on us until the wash of dawnlight lifts the sky and sends my body withering.

Darius's face is startled, exhausted when I rise to meet him, oblivious that the sky came down on us like a fist. I exhale. I had a turbulent dream—a nightmare among the stars—and that's all. I'm no Terry Combs. I'm composed. My mouth peels like velcro and my brain taps against my skull but I know who I am and what I have to do.

"There's a brewery around here," I say to Darius. His expression tightens. The budding light grants his bald head a halo. "For Alvin. Let's do it for Alvin."

Alvin shuffles in his sleeping bag. He groans. "Please."

"You heard him," I say to Darius. "The guy wants to go."

"That was more of a begging 'please,' you know."

"I beg to differ."

Darius throws his hands up in defeat. I'm saving the trip. Throwing its fractured body over my shoulder. My body is wrung out. Last night was the delicate delirium between sleep and consciousness and I do not know if I dreamed. My dreams after drinking—which is a little frequent—either fall into blackout void or are so vivid they're tangible. I'm no Terry Combs. I'm together. I tell myself that again. On the road back I witness the beauty of the Mendocino landscape, the blonde Californian hills that fold into each other. I realize the road to the Lost Coast is not a good one, the ribbon—laced with potholes and hairpin turns and signs with bullet holes—tears through the countryside, and the land in turn spills dirt and sends tree roots that hack the pavement.

Darius says something but the road comes to a new patch of asphalt, stitched into the old quilt that causes the car to go silent, wheels gliding over the soft black strip. I tune out, closing my eyes, listen to the world holding its breath.

"Drive us safe," Darius echoes far off. When I open my eyes the road bottoms out to gravel and dust. Darius curses. Alvin's head thumps the back of Darius's seat. We fishtail then straighten, I whoop, and the rig barrels along the Lost Coast in a pluming brown wake.

My hangover is bellowing at full roar when we pull up to the brewery. Alvin and Darius order a beer; I order a flight, small several ounce tasters of each of the brewery's beers. Instead of smelling the aromatics and sipping, I rip them like shots, starting with the highest in alcohol content and working my way down to lift me up from sober reprieve. My brain still feels a spongy basketball crammed into my small head.

"You don't have any liquor by chance?"

"Sorry," says the waitress. "Just beer."

She comes back with a round of pints. When I'm halfway through mine, Alvin's seat is vacant and his beer stands untouched, the head of foam melting into a tall blonde body. The residual webbing of beer slides down my glass. Darius docks his head in his elbow. I put my glass down.

"Another round," I say, twirling my finger in the air.

"I can't give your table another round until all those beers are gone."

I rouse Darius and guzzle Alvin's beer. I tell the waitress to bring two beers and to have the third on deck.

When the pints land, a light goes out in the corner. I clang glasses with Darius. I'm no Terry Combs. I tilt his glass from the bottom and watch his throat bob to take it all in. The liquid streams out of the corners of the glass, down his throat, and into his collar. I realize what I'm doing is shitty but he's not furious. He sets his glass down and says, "I'm too drunk to drive."

That's fine. Ideal, actually. Going back to San Francisco is the last thing I want to do. I turn around for the waitress. I see my finger twirling in the air above me. The place has definitely dimmed. The walls darken to orange and the tables are empty.

"Another round."

"How are you going to pay for this?"

"Put it on the plastic," I say, trying to sling Darius's credit card suavely but throwing it like a frisbee across the room. She fetches it from the floor.

"How are we going to get back? How can we go home?" I hear Darius ask, far off. When I turn around he's not in his seat. The lights behind the bar go out one by one, the staccato of clicks punctuating the tap room. There's no music playing and I'm soaked in the silence of the darkening bar. Water starts to rise from the floorboards. I call for a mop. One of the walls gives way and the hills burst in. The asphalt ribbon is diced to confetti and the innocuous gold stalks sway. I wave back. Holy dust filters in around the tables. My mouth starts to dry and my tongue sticks to the walls of my mouth. As the tap room slides into the ocean the opposite wall distends and then ruptures, drowning my waist. My wallet floats to a tree that sprouts behind the bar. "Good riddance," I say. More light bulbs go out, this time exploding in ornery pops until the sole light above our table palpitates. Holy dust becomes mud. Everything is going down around me. The water crawls up my neck and the brine tickles my nose. A bathtub cruises by. "Another round!" I holler as the sea foam inundates my mouth and consumes my head, my beckoning finger breaches rising tide, still doing laps in the air.

Mistress Winter

Shilo Niziolek

I'm waiting for the sheets of ice to cover the ground,
for the icicles to drip from the picnic table,
the power pole, the mailboxes, and trees that line the street.
The ice will be so biting
that trees over fifty years old
will tear out their roots
just to shatter the pieces on the ground.
There will be floods
racing to see who can be the first to drown out the rest of us.
When the waters rage and the rain pours for days on end
will we finally learn how to cry?
We need winter this year;
The hollow gutting out of the land,
the stripped trees, the tower of blankets
as we huddle into our own darkness.
Our emptiness tight from all the sweating.
We don't need a gentle cleanse
But a rough and raging detox.
We need the winds to whip through the land,
The plants to bow to its glory.
The whisper as it puts us to sleep.

Irene Ritley

My Friend's Mother

John P. Kristofco

an apparition at the door
in summer when we spread like fire
in the neighborhood,
skinny as a painted vein,
hair more red than it should ever be,
cigarette as always in her mouth,
this hawk-faced harpie
flashing eyes from one thing
to the next,
looking for her children in the yard,
listening for voices from across the street,
and when she couldn't see or hear,
she'd scream out like a siren:
"MICHAEL JAMES!!" exploded like a rocket
from the rusted metal door,
a puff of smoke like gunshot from her lips
and so, my best friend's feral reverie
was captured,
and we were called to 'reason'
by the warrant of his mother
once again

Diaspora

Lance Nizami

The sweet one the warm one my loving one has flown away

Three nights I sleep alone beneath synthetic bunny-fur, three nights
My sweet one too will sleep alone, a mini childhood stuffed-toy by
    her side
She sleeps in childhood bed in childhood home in childhood 'burb of
    childhood town
The suburb has not changed though newer cars sit in the driveways

Some folks are older some much older; homes remain the same

Gone the young the sweet the warm the loving ones they flew away
They flew away and nested somewhere else where jobs were found big
    cities other lands
They flew to places having lesser cold less snow less ice and lower taxes
Returning they returned each time to carry forth a casket

Each time a time of cold and ice and snow upon the ground

Each time a time for steaming coffee heavy coats and gloves outdoors
Each time a time for reminiscing over donuts maple-iced

Each time a time to sleep once more in childhood bed in childhood
home

Each time a time for someone left alone elsewhere to sleep beneath
synthetic bunny-fur

The sweet one the warm one my loving one has flown away

Ritual

Paulann Petersen

—for my grandfather, Archie Theobald (1890–1955)

Sundays, you didn't work, your fur shop
silent. In its front window, the CLOSED sign
turned itself neatly toward the traffic
on Sandy Boulevard. Any Sunday,
I might have been staying with you and Nana,
there for the weekend. Every Sunday, the *Oregonian*
arrived on your front porch, thick and weighted
with the ink of extra ads. Sunday's comics
were printed in color—Slugo and Sparkle Plenty
wearing deep, bright hues.

                We looked at the paper—
you, the front section—me, *Parade* and the comics—
and when we were done, I carried
its bulk away. In a stack by the back porch door,
I found Saturday's paper, skimpy and by then
in slip-shod folds, curling at its edges. I turned
to its comic strip page and smoothed it out
on the chrome-edged kitchen table. I fetched
your box of colored pencils, a whole Faber set

with every basic color—as well as
the rare ones in between.

In black and white,
Saturday's comics were starkly drawn,
each character and object outlined
in ink, those wan spaces in every panel
waiting for us resident artists. Little Orphan Annie
got her red hair. Dick Tracy's suit shouldered
its detective blue. Trees leafed out. Skies cleared.
In Prince Valiant's crown the jewels
grew precious. Veronica put on lipstick.
Blondie bespoke her name.

Now that I've lived
for years beyond the age at which you died,
I see—more clearly than ever—those Sundays.
You sit at the kitchen table, me at your side,
our heads together, bowed to our work.
Your slacks are charcoal, your shirt beige.
The metal parts of your wheelchair, silver.
In your fingers a cigar gleams
its bronzed brown, the lit end flaring
into ember-red each time you take a puff.
As you exhale, your breath becomes
the color of smoke. In slow swirls,
it eases upward, meanders the air,
leaving its trace below—
that ghost

of steel-gray ash.

The Mother-Son Dance

Paul Brownsey

The way I got my mother to attend my wedding was as follows.

There was always an undercurrent between her and my Uncle Ron. Oh, she and my dad, when he was around, used to exchange visits with Uncle Ron and his wife, because that was what families did. There were Christmas cards between them, properly signed *with our love* but all that was just on the surface.

Once, when their sister was in hospital after one of her breakdowns, Mum, who cleaned house for a posh woman, persuaded the woman to drive her to visit Rosie. The minute she got back, she was on the phone to Uncle Ron. "I know I can't afford a car but I thought it my duty to go. It was three hundred miles round trip. I don't think you're as far as that from Rosie, are you? I've not really measured it on the map." The voice sounded so innocent. "Rosie was so pleased to see someone from the family."

"Perhaps his arm is bothering him too much to drive long distances," I said when she'd put the phone down. He has a building firm and a pile of timber once fell on the arm.

"Ah, I didn't know his arm is bothering him."

"I didn't say it *is* bothering him. I only said *perhaps*. Mentioning it as a possibility."

"No, I didn't know his arm is bothering him."

When Rosie got out of hospital, Mum saw another opportunity for martyrdom and had her to stay with us to recuperate. I thought she'd try to get me to give up my bedroom and sleep in the living room, but she had Rosie to sleep with her in her bed and went around saying, "Here's us squeezed up like sardines and Ron all by himself in that big house since Vera died." She'd laugh as if it was no more than amusing.

Auntie Vera died young of a brain haemorrhage and they hadn't had children. I became, for Uncle Ron, the son he'd never had. What he did later to get Mum to my wedding proves it. There was something reassuring in his burly figure and his patient, thoughtful face with its heavy glasses. He'd have me to stay in the school holidays, and I got treats and outings Mum couldn't afford after my dad ran off. He'd take days off from his building firm and we'd go to the seaside, kicking a ball about on the beach like two boys, or to the zoo or museums. He'd point out a strange animal or a weird mask or a painting and say, "What do you think of that?"—not because he had things to say about them, because he hadn't, but just because he liked listening to my replies. One birthday, there was a huge electric train-set from him, with two locos, yards of track, branch lines, a model station, etc. From Mum I got a pen-knife with gadgets on it. "Don't know why you want to spend that amount of money on a boy who's not your own son. It's not good for him, presents like that," I heard her tell him, making me wonder if the electricity would make worse my chesty childhood illnesses, though that didn't stop me whizzing the trains through junctions. To me, she said, "If he's so fond of you why doesn't he buy your shoes and school uniform and things while I'm working two jobs to pay for them? That'd be more use than train sets that use up electricity."

One of her biggest rows with Uncle Ron was over their mother's money. There wasn't a will. He said it was only fair to divide the money three ways between himself, Mum and Rosie. Mum said Rosie wasn't capable of looking after money and she should get Rosie's share "on a trust" to use for Rosie's good.

I heard her shout at Uncle Ron, "She's got a screw loose. She has breakdowns like other people have colds and I have to pick up the bloody pieces." The nastiness was a shocking contrast to the tenderness I remembered in her voice when, ushering Rosie through our door after one of her hospital episodes, Mum said, "You're safe now, you poor dear." Later, an odd thought sometimes pecked at me: is there such a thing as a reverse hypocrite, someone who says awful things but whose actions are the opposite?

In the end, Rosie's share was made over to her after Uncle Ron contacted a lawyer. "Bringing in a lawyer!" Mum said to me, like he'd desecrated holy ground. "I don't know how he had the face." Soon afterwards, Rosie had a religious conversion, standing in the shopping mall singing hymns and doing what she said was speaking in tongues, laughing when the security men led her away. She gave her share of the money to her church, where, Mum's *Daily Mail* later revealed, the pastor used the congregation's offerings to buy houses in his own name for rent. He let Rosie have a flatlet in one of them but she couldn't afford the rent so he threw her out, and Mum and I had another period of Rosie living with us.

When I told Mum that Philip and I were getting married, she flinched and said, "Oh no!" in the strained, stopped-breathing voice she uses to convey: *This is yet another blow.* I can't say her mouth turned down, because it's always turned down, like she's being continually slighted and resents it.

"I suppose it's just one more thing for me to put up with. Sister with a screw loose. Your father running off with that woman." As always, I had a momentary picture of them leaping fences, hand in hand, the woman's face blanked out. "And now I have a son ruining his life."

"You've known for years I'm gay."

"I don't like that word. No, I *don't*." She spoke as though people were trying to persuade her she did like it. "I thought it was just silliness, that sort of thing."

"Silliness? It's so *not* silly, that I live with Philip. You've spent two Christmas Days at our place. Remember?"

"*I* thought he was just a nice friend helping you to be sensible again." Her emphasis on the first word in that sentence declared that what she thought was the authoritative view, outranking anything even I might say to the contrary. "Even though he does work in your Uncle Ron's offices."

That was where I'd met him. Uncle Ron was about to introduce us but was called away to the phone. Philip stretched his long, slim body backwards at the desk where he saw to the legal and planning side of things; gave me a quiet, unsettling stare and said, "So, Ian, where are we going for a drink tonight?" It was the first thing he ever said to me. For once, it wasn't irritating when someone began speaking with "So" because here it felt like he'd known me for ages and was merely spelling out something that had been implicit between us forever. Then he gave the cheerful schoolboy grin he can do.

I told Mum, "Well, we're getting married, and that's that." I tried for lightness. "So you'll have to get yourself a new outfit and a big picture hat."

"After all I've done for you, bringing you up alone after your father ran off with that woman. And it was him that wanted kids. And have you thought about this AIDS? I remember the adverts. It'll be me you come running to. I'm the one that cares for people in this family. No, don't expect *me* to be there. Your father and I got married *properly.*"

"Didn't stop him leaving you," I couldn't bring myself to say.

Nor could I say, as in an American TV drama, "But I love you, Mom, and I need you there on the most important day of my life!"

I just said, "Suit yourself."

I told Uncle Ron, "Worse than I expected. An absolute No."

He could see I was upset and pressed my shoulder. "We'll still make it a great day without her. You've got Philip, that's the main thing. Good-looking guy, too." He laughed and pulled Philip to him and stood with one arm around my shoulders, one around Philip's. "My two boys are going to have a day to remember."

He squeezed both sets of shoulders until I pulled away. "She thinks I'll get AIDS if we get married. She's never forgotten those adverts about AIDS, what was it, thirty-odd years ago? What can you say to someone who thinks like she does?"

Uncle Ron said, "There's no point in my speaking to her."

"Actually, there could be." I found I was trying to give him a quiet stare like Philip's.

When I'd explained, he said, "Well, since I'm paying for the reception, I suppose that's as good as being there," which showed how much he loved me.

Mum phoned me. "I'm not having it. Do you know what your precious Ron's saying about you?"

"What?" I wailed it, for I don't like lying and that way I avoided answering her question.

"He refuses to attend a dirty little imitation wedding, he said. A perverted and unnatural something-or-other. What a thing to say! You always thought he was wonderful, because of the train sets and gallivanting. It was a mercy Vera died when she did, the things that came out after. He says, I hope *you're* not going to this wedding. Telling me not to attend my own son's wedding! He's my son, not yours, I said." Her voice expected me to be pleased she'd stuck up for me.

"Still, he's only telling you not to do what you're not going to do anyway."

"We'll see about that," she said as she rang off, in the voice in which, when I was a boy, she'd declared war on my headmaster over my being punished for something I hadn't done.

She phoned me again. "So what about the Mother-Son dance?"

"I think that's more of an American thing," I began, but I didn't want to send her back into refusal mode, so I said, "But, yes, why not? Let's do it!" I put special intimacy into the last three words, and she reminded me, "I taught you to waltz." My 10-year-old hand, cautiously on her hip, had been aware of her girdle as she pulled me around the living room while she la-la'd *The Anniversary Song,* losing herself in the song as though I was as expert a partner as Fred Astaire, enfolding me in the cool scent of the *eau de cologne* that she used both for perfume and for headaches.

"*Sunrise, Sunset* is what they do, isn't it?" she added. "From that musical. All about Jews."

I reported to Philip: "It's all settled, she's coming. No explicit climb-down but she's hooked on the idea of the Mother-Son dance."

"I don't suppose my mother would be up for that because it'll be right after her knee replacement, but I'll ask her. She likes *Strictly.*"

"Oh, no! Philip, please. Mum'll be picturing her and me twirling alone while everyone *Oohs* and *Ahs.* That's how it would be if it was the wedding she wanted. She might back out if…" I couldn't put it into words.

"There are two sons in this wedding, Ian."

I thought he was going to refuse, but then his quiet stare was succeeded by his nice-kid grin, and he said, "Okay. You can dance to *And His Mother Came, Too*."

Since he loved me enough to climb down on that, I decided to take advantage of the moment.

"Can I ask that, when the registrar says we're married, we don't kiss? I don't think she would walk out, but she might say something like 'Oh, no!' in that way she has, like she's suffering a blow."

When he just stared, and the almost-neutralising grin didn't follow, I hastened to engage his sense of responsibility to others. "It's not me I'm thinking of. Her saying that would embarrass everyone; make everyone anxious about what was coming next." He gave a flicker of an eye-roll but, "Yes," he said, "Okay."

...Someone announced the first dance of the evening. "And it's a special one, for two special people: *Sunrise, Sunset*." Philip's voice, I realised. Mum was occupying a little table with Rosie, who'd earlier stood up during the ceremony, hair purple-streaked, full-length green dress like a priestess's, a necklace of what looked like clam shells, and declared Philip and I were predestined to be happy because we were mentioned in the Bible—"The book of Philipp-Ians." I said, "Mum, it's time for *us*," putting my special-intimacy emphasis on *us*.

As she got to her feet, she said to someone at the next table, "He's a good boy, in spite of it all."

Her dress was slightly above knee-length in some slinky orange material, and her startling lipstick matched. This wasn't exactly mother-at-the-wedding attire. Could the prospective presence of so many men have re-awakened an old instinct to attract? Certainly, the way she'd held herself as she stood surveying Philip's and my gay friends, one arm dangling her handbag negligently by its strap, the other hand touching her face in a pose of thoughtfulness as her gaze moved from one to the other, might lead you to suspect an intention to overcome their silliness and be noticed. The dress might also be meant to confer *Strictly*-style pizzazz on her moment in the limelight in the Mother-Son dance. Its fringed hem revealed shapely, agile legs for which a dance was a serious business. "Your dad and I used to win dance competitions. Such a shame he can't be here to see us."

In appearance, I led; in reality she did, her dancing skill masking my clumsiness. The fortress girdle of old was no more, her breasts were mobile against me, and her hips seemed to sway more assertively than the music required. Dancing with girls in my teenage years, I'd felt alarm at being totally void of any inclination to continue holding my partner after the dance was over, and now, weirdly, that old alarm revisited me. I wondered whether she had danced with my father like this and produced in him a different reaction.

Suddenly there was another couple on the floor.

Naturally, I wouldn't fail to recognise Philip's long body inside his formal clothes. For a moment, I thought he must be dancing with his mother after all, having considerately given me and Mum the limelight first.

But his partner, holding him close in ballroom hold, was a man: tall, powerful-bodied, with heavy, dark-framed glasses; Uncle Ron.

Who, we'd settled, wasn't going to attend.

"Oh, no!" said Mum. I held her closer to prevent her walking off the floor, releasing a gust of *eau de cologne* that made me realise that beneath its association with headaches, it could be the perfume of passion, too. She responded to my tighter hold with some particularly lively turns.

"What does that man think he's up to? It's silliness. Two men dancing together. Ron spoiling your big moment."

"He loves me so much he wasn't able to stay away," I wanted to say, but didn't.

Uncle Ron and Philip came closer, circling round us as though closing in on prey. Mum shut her eyes and hummed *Sunrise, Sunset* like a charm against everything unpleasant, and then Philip tapped me on the shoulder and said, "This is a gentleman's excuse-me." Mum went to move into his arms but he sidestepped her, took hold of me, and waltzed me away. His hand in the small of my back entirely banished my self-consciousness and suddenly I felt married and wanted to hold on to him forever. I kissed him as we danced, and all the people sitting around the edge of the room clapped and whooped and cheered.

But as I kissed him my eyes were on the other pair. Mum and Uncle Ron looked uncertainly at each other, then Uncle Ron made a courteous sweeping movement and said, "Donalda!" Her lips turned upwards in a smile that gave her face the sweetness of a young girl's and made you think that that was what she was truly like. She allowed him to take her in his arms, and then they were dancing, too. None of the spectators seemed at all puzzled by what had happened. Rosie caught my eye and waved. In a gesture of triumph she held aloft the marble ornament she'd given us as a wedding present, carved in a Celtic design that, all excited, she'd told us was a fertility symbol.

Walking on the Beach
and Thinking about My Father

Charles Tarlton

> *It's in many ways*
> *a relief to have you dead.*
>
> —Frank Bidart

I am now the age my father was when he was old
and the sky today was the same gray as the sea

he said it was art, the guy with the colored chalk
smudging the sidewalk

he made rainbows with nine striped bands
the ocean was yellow

Sand in the wind hits like pellets
blown along ahead of the waves; from the sea

a silver bracelet wound around in promises like vines
envelope an ancient oak; the oak stands coyly admiring itself

I tried to make a ring in the water with a thrown stone
wind itself around rings radiating from a stone already thrown

sparks and radio waves off the tower on the world
send a message—*di-di-di-dah*—to the edges of the screen

the sun going down into the sea is like earth's eye slowly winking
you look around for the joke but it keeps on getting dark

I may in fact be older than my father was when he was old

Road to the Sky

John Sibley Williams

The pictures on my wall have
passed their expiration date. Holy
ones first. Now grandparents. My
children and the children I hope
they have. At a certain point the
room and then the whole world
sours if left uneaten. Complete.
Clouds coagulate, thicken. Stars
green on the pond. A few can't
muster sky anymore. My neighbor
still drinks and bathes in the sacred
urine cows empty in a country he's
lost too much of the language to
remember. We have horses out
here. We have floods. Huge boats.
His father spent fifty five years
conducting snakes for tourists to
gasp and awe and ask if his is
maybe the better god. I try not to
think about the half of me that's
elephant. The half vulture. And all
that's dead. Can't there be a single

room without an exit? Just one road
that does not *pass for* but radiates
ruin. I can see the stone saints'
mouths moving around some
unutterable word. They're scattering
chicken bones below my window
now. They're placing bets on the
live ones. Even when sated, it seems
we can make any body edible.

Oblations

Marie Louise St.Onge

Thank you little bird for being
a little bird, for singing on the bleakest morning.
And you, brilliant dandelion for shining your bright light
yellow all day long.
My gratitude to the black cat and the leaning ladder
for being in front of me.
To my mother's bad uncle who trained me to keep secrets
I extend one small nod.
And to my aunt, my very favorite aunt, who explained
elocution to me and recognized I needed it.
My remembrance, too, to the nun who announced
(with me sitting in the classroom) that my brother was going blind.

To the faraway train and its horn that blows low in the sleepless night
thank you for the sweet call home.
For the French I've managed to remember despite my own neglect
c'est une bonne plaisir la voix comme la musique.
To the stinging single malt that whispers down my throat
I'll lean on you but only so much.
And for the spoon's gentle curve and her generous delivery
of winter's hot soup, my appreciation.
To the cards that fall from the shuffler's hand

when good fate follows, and for the one single star
that brights the night thank you
for leading the way.

I love the spade that rests in the dirt
all furrows in place, and the great mounds of white piled high
in drifts following February's mood.
To the burst of sun after rain and snow
and for the sweetness of wasting compost.
For birthday cakes that mark the years
as they tick tock by,
to the grave that waits where I will rest my bones—
good, I will have earned you.
And to my mother,
who tried and worried
always in some shadow, I understand.

Remodeling the kitchen won't expand your mind

Ying Wu

My fellow law-abiding citizens—
as we steer our carts
through Costco and Walmart
and Target and Best Buy,
let us remember this:
We are somewhere.
Inside our shoes.
Between the cans of soup
and bags of noodles.
Between crossing off sanitizer
and searching for arugula.
Between the chill of dawn
and the cool of night.
Between apex and nadir.
Between the arc of the sky
and our parking spots.

We are more than 7 billion in the world.
Each one of us is somewhere.
The bones of our forefathers are somewhere.

Our baby bonnet buttons,

the old TV's we forsook for flat screens,

the prizes from our Happy Meals—are somewhere.

My law-abiding brothers and sisters,

as we dream frontiers from our cul-de-sacs,

and pull the crab grass,

and whiten our teeth,

I ask of you this: Touch your navel.

We came into life through connection.

Feel the soles of your feet—

We are somewhere.

We are here.

Contributors

Jeffrey Alfier's recent books include *Fugue for a Desert Mountain*, *Anthem for Pacific Avenue*, and *The Red Stag at Carrbridge: Scotland Poems*. His publication credits include *Copper Nickel*, *Meridian*, *Midwest Quarterly*, *Poetry Ireland Review*, and *The McNeese Review*. He is founder of Blue Horse Press and *San Pedro River Review*.

Pat Anthony writes from the rural midwest. Recently retired from education, she continues to mine the furrows both in the land and in the faces of those who work it. She has work published or forthcoming in *Cholla Needles*, *Waterways*, *San Pedro River Review*, *Fourth & Sycamore*, and *Open Minds Quarterly*, among others.

Devon Balwit teaches in Portland, OR. She has six chapbooks and two collections out or forthcoming: *How the Blessed Travel* (Maverick Duck Press); *Forms Most Marvelous* (dancing girl press); *In Front of the Elements* (Grey Borders Books), *Where You Were Going Never Was* (Grey Borders Books); *The Bow Must Bear the Brunt* (Red Flag Poetry); *We are Procession, Seismograph* (Nixes Mate Books), *Risk Being/Complicated* (with the Canadian artist Lorette C. Luzajic), and *Motes at Play in the Halls of Light* (Kelsay Books). Her individual poems can be found in *Cordite*, *The Cincinnati Review*, *The Carolina Quarterly*, *Fifth Wednesday*, *Red Earth Review*, *The Fourth River*, *The Free State Review*, *Rattle*, *The Inflectionist Review*, *Posit*, and more.

Paul Brownsey lives in Scotland and is a former member of the Philosophy faculty at Glasgow University. His book, *His Steadfast Love and Other Stories*, was published by Lethe Press, NJ, received a starred review in *Publishers Weekly*, and was a finalist in the Lambda Literary Awards.

S.W. Campbell was born in Eastern Oregon. He currently resides in Portland where he works as an economist and lives with a house plant named Morton. Attack is his fifteenth short story to be published. It, as well as numerous short stories, will be available in his first short story collection, *An Unsated Thirst*, this summer. He is also the author of a book, *The Uncanny Valley*, and runs a historical satire blog called *Professor Errare Presents*.

James Deahl was born in Pittsburgh in 1945, and grew up in that city as well as in the Laurel Highlands region of the Appalachian Mountains. He is the author of twenty-seven literary titles, the five most recent being: *Red Haws To Light The Field* (2017), *To Be With A Woman* (2016), *Landscapes* (with Katherine L. Gordon, 2016), *Unbroken Lines* (2015), and *Two Paths Through The Seasons* (with Norma West Linder, 2014). A cycle of his poems is the focus of a one-hour TV special, *Under the Watchful Eye* (Silver Falls Video Productions, 1993). The audiotape of *Under the Watchful Eye* was released by Broken Jaw Press in 1995. These have been reissued on CD and DVD by Silver Falls. Since 1970 he has lived in Canada where he writes and edits full-time. Deahl is the father of Sarah, Simone, and Shona, and grandfather of Rebekah.

Jack Donahue has written numerous short stories and poems that have been published in journals such as: *Newtown Literary Review*,

Clackamas Literary Review, Lullwater Review, Palo Alto Review, The Main Street Rag, China Grove, Folio, The Almagre Review, and others throughout North America and Europe. Mr. Donahue received his M.Div. degree from New Brunswick, Theological Seminary, NJ, in 2008. He is married and resides on the North Fork of Long Island, NY.

Jennifer Dorner's poetry has appeared in or is forthcoming from *Chicago Quarterly Review, Sugar House Review, The Inflectionist Review, Cloudbank, The Timberline Review, Verseweavers,* and *VoiceCatcher.* Jennifer was selected as a finalist in the Ruth Stone Poetry Prize in 2016 and was a finalist in the Hedgebrook 2018 Writers in Residence Program. She is currently a MFA student at Pacific University.

Lawrence F. Farrar is a former U.S. diplomat with multiple assignments in Japan as well as postings in Germany, Norway, and Washington, DC. He also lived in Japan as a graduate student and as a naval officer. His stories have appeared 60 or so times in lit magazines, such as *The Chaffin Journal, Zone 3, Streetlight, Curbside Splendor E-Zine, Evening Street Review, Big Muddy, Tampa Review Online, O-Dark-Thirty, Jelly Bucket, The MacGuffin,* and *Green Hills Literary Lantern.* His stories often involve people coming up against the customs of a foreign culture.

Benjamin McPherson Ficklin was born in Portland, OR, but now spends most of his life travelling. Outside of his writing and photography, he works as a gongfu tea-master, lumberjack, commercial salmon fisherman, and ulu farmer. His work has been published in *Lomography, Ursus Americanus Press, Autre, Oregon Voice Magazine,* and all three anthologies by The StoneCutters Union.

Kathleen Hellen is the author of the collection *Umberto's Night*, winner of the Jean Feldman Poetry Prize, and two chapbooks, *The Girl Who Loved Mothra* and *Pentimento*. Her poems have appeared in *American Letters and Commentary*, *Barrow Street*, *The Massachusetts Review*, *New Letters*, *North American Review*, *Poetry East*, *Seattle Review*, the *Sewanee Review*, *Spoon River Poetry Review*, *Witness*, and elsewhere. Nominated for the Pushcart and Best of the Net, and featured on Poetry Daily, her poems have been awarded the Thomas Merton poetry prize and prizes from the *H.O.W. Journal* and *Washington Square Review*.

Andrea Hollander moved to Portland, OR, in 2011, after many years in the Arkansas Ozark Mountains, where she ran a bed & breakfast for 15 years and served as the Writer-in-Residence at Lyon College for 22. Her poems and essays have appeared in numerous anthologies, college textbooks, and literary journals. Hollander's 5th full-length poetry collection, *Blue Mistaken as Sky*, will be released by Autumn House in September 2018. Her 4th collection was a finalist for the Oregon Book Award; her 1st won the Nicholas Roerich Poetry Prize. Among her many other honors are the 2017 Vern Rutsala Award, a 2013 Oregon Literary Fellowship, two Pushcart Prizes (in poetry and literary nonfiction) and two poetry fellowships from the National Endowment of the Arts.

Daniel M. Jaffe is author of the new novel, *Yeled Tov* (2018); the novel-in-stories, *The Genealogy of Understanding* (2014); the collection, *Jewish Gentle and Other Stories of Gay-Jewish Living* (2011); and the novel, *The Limits of Pleasure* (2010). Several of his short stories have been nominated for a Pushcart Prize.

John P. Kristofco has published poetry and short stories in about two hundred publications, including *Folio, Rattle, Cimarron Review, Blueline, Slant, Fourth River, Chiron Review, Snowy Egret,* and *Poem* (where his work has appeared in each of the last five decades). He has published three poetry chapbooks (recently, *The Timekeeper's Garden* (The Orchard Street Press, orchpress.com) with a fourth, *Portraits From the Pilgrimage,* due out this summer. Jack has been nominated for the Pushcart Prize five times. A retired professor of English and college dean at The University of Akron, Jack lives in Highland Heights with his wife Kathy.

Mercedes Lawry has published poetry in such journals as *Poetry, Nimrod, Prairie Schooner,* and *Harpur Palate.* Thrice-nominated for a Pushcart Prize, she's published two chapbooks. Her manuscript "Small Measures" was selected for the Vachel Lindsay Poetry Prize from Twelve Winters Press and will be published in 2018. She was a finalist for the 2017 Airlie Press Prize and the 2017 Wheelbarrow Press Book Prize. She's also published short fiction, essays as well as stories and poems for children. She lives in Seattle.

Donald Levering's 7th full-length poetry book, *Coltrane's God,* published in 2015 by Red Mountain Press, was runner-up for the New England Book Festival contest. His previous book, *The Water Leveling with Us,* placed second in the 2015 National Federation of Press Women Creative Verse Competition. He is a former NEA Fellow and won the 2014 Literal Latté award and the 2017 Tor House Robinson Jeffers Prize.

Sue Mach's plays have been produced by Theatre for the New City in Manhattan, Bloomsburg Theatre Ensemble, Portland Repertory The-

atre, CoHo Theatre, Artists Repertory Theatre, Portland World The-
atre, Third Rail, and Icarus Theatre Ensemble. She has been teaching
literature, composition, and digital storytelling classes at Clackamas
Community College for the past twenty years.

Lance Nizami has more than 240 poems in print in recognized poetry
journals, some recent publications being in *Eastern Structures* and in
Pilgrimage.

Shilo Niziolek lives in Portland, OR, with her partner Andrew and their
two dogs. She is currently studying Creative Writing and English Litera-
ture at Marylhurst University. Her work has been published in the *Broad
River Review*, the *M Review*, Z Publishing's *Oregon's Best Emerging
Poets Anthology*, *The Gateway Review*, and is forthcoming in *Heart-
wood Literary Magazine* and *SLAB*. When not writing or devouring
books, she spends her time trying to discover the language of ferns.

Akachi Obijiaku is a new Nigerian poet who started writing poetry
in 2017. Her works are forthcoming or appearing across ten literary
journals. She emigrated to England four years ago and holds an MSc
from King's College London.

Nate Orton is an artist, printer and educator living in Portland, OR.
Currently he is working on the 43rd issue of his chapbook, *My Day*,
which explores the Pacific Northwest through drawing, writing, and
traditional as well as non-traditional printmaking techniques. Nate
teaches visual art at the Multnomah Arts Center and is a candidate for
a Masters of Arts in Teaching at Concordia University, Portland. Nate
attempts to draw daily. Most days are a success.

Ricardo Pau-Llosa's eighth book of poems due this fall from Carnegie Mellon, his longtime publisher. He has also published widely on the visual arts. *Intruder between Rivers/Intruso entre ríos*, a limited edition of an artisan-produced book gathering 25 previously published poems with facing-page translations into Spanish by Enrico Mario Santí, was recently published by Del Centro Editores, Madrid.

Simon Perchik is an attorney whose poems have appeared in *Partisan Review*, *Forge*, *Poetry*, *Osiris*, *The New Yorker*, and elsewhere. His most recent collection is *The Osiris Poems* published by Box of Chalk, 2017.

Paulann Petersen, Oregon Poet Laureate Emerita, has six full-length books of poetry: *The Wild Awake*, *Blood-Silk*, *A Bride of Narrow Escape*, *Kindle*, *The Voluptuary*, and most recently *Understory*, from Lost Horse Press in 2013. "A Blueprint of That Vaster Blue" and "Ritual" are poems in *One Small Sun*, a seventh collection forthcoming from Salmon Press of Ireland in March of 2019. Her poems have appeared in many journals and anthologies, including *Poetry*, *The New Republic*, *Prairie Schooner*, *Notre Dame Review*, *Wilderness Magazine*, the *Internet's Poetry Daily*, and *POETRY IN MOTION*, which places poems on the TriMet busses and lightrail cars in the Portland area. The Latvian composer Eriks Esenvalds chose a poem from her book *The Voluptuary* as the lyric for a new choral composition that's now part of the repertoire of the Choir at Trinity College Cambridge.

Stephen R. Roberts collects books, geodes, gargoyles, poetic lariats, and various other objects of interest to enhance his basic perceptions of a chaotic planet that pays little attention to him, as far as he knows. He's had poems published in *Rain City Review*, *Sulfur River Review*,

Blackwater, Black River Review, Talking River, WaterStone, River-run, Connecticut River Review, and, to get away from all the moisture, *Dry Creek Review.* He has been nominated twice for a Pushcart Prize and has five published chapbooks. His full length work, *Almost Music From Between Places,* is available from Chatter House Press.

Lex Runciman's sixth book, *Salt Moons: Poems 1981–2016,* was published in 2017 by Salmon Poetry. An earlier volume won the Oregon Book Award. Now retired, he lives in Portland, OR.

Michael J. Shymanski was born in San Francisco and studied creative writing at the University of San Francisco. His writing has been featured in *Forth Magazine, Broke-Ass Stuart,* and *Timber Journal.* He currently lives in Portland, where he is a contributing editor of bilingual literary magazine, *Frontera* based in Madrid and Portland.

Marie Louise St.Onge's writing has appeared in literary magazines across the country including *Yankee Magazine, Permafrost, Potato Eyes, Café Review, Rafale: Revue Litteraire,* and others. She is the Executive Editor of *Ad Hoc Monadnock—A Literary Anthology;* a former editor for *The Worcester Review;* and a contributor to *French Class: French Canadian-American Writings on Identity, Culture and Place.* Marie Louise has read her poetry at universities, art and community centers, and bookstores throughout New England.

Sabrina Stout is a Clackamas Community College alumnus and lives in Clackamas, OR. She is currently studying Spanish, English, and writing at Portland State University, where she will graduate with a BA in May, 2019. This is her first publication.

Charles Tarlton is a retired university professor from New York currently living (and writing poetry and flash prose) in western Massachusetts with his wife, Ann Knickerbocker, an abstract painter. In the last decade or so he has published just enough of his work to keep him in the game.

John Sibley Williams is the editor of two Northwest poetry anthologies and the author of nine collections, including *Disinheritance* and *Controlled Hallucinations*. An eleven-time Pushcart nominee, John is the winner of numerous awards, including the Philip Booth Award, American Literary Review Poetry Contest, Nancy D. Hargrove Editors' Prize, Confrontation Poetry Prize, and Vallum Award for Poetry. He serves as editor of *The Inflectionist Review* and works as a literary agent. Previous publishing credits include: *The Yale Review, Midwest Quarterly, Sycamore Review, Prairie Schooner, The Massachusetts Review, Poet Lore, Saranac Review, Atlanta Review, TriQuarterly, Columbia Poetry Review, Mid-American Review, Poetry Northwest, Third Coast*, and various anthologies. He lives in Portland, OR.

Ying Wu studies neurocognitive mechanisms mediating creativity and insight and hosts San Diego's Gelato Poetry Series. Her work has been featured in *Serving House Journal, Synesthesia Anthology, Blue Heron Review, The San Diego Poetry Annual*, and *The Poetry Superhighway*, and was awarded honorable mention in the Kowit poetry competition.

The *Clackamas Literary Review* is typeset in Sabon LT Std, an old-style serif designed by Jan Tschichold, and in Optima, a humanistic sans-serif designed by Hermann Zapf, and printed on 50 lb. white paper. Editing and design done by English Department students and faculty at Clackamas Community College, in Oregon City, Oregon.

Visit

CLR

CLACKAMAS LITERARY REVIEW

clackamasliteraryreview.org
clackamasliteraryreview.submittable.com
facebook.com/clackamasliteraryreview
@clackamaslitrev

Contact
clr@clackamas.edu

CLACKAMAS LITERARY REVIEW

the finest writing for the best readers

Clackamas Literary Review has been committed to publishing quality writing from around the world since 1997. Use the form below or visit us on Submittable to receive the latest and forthcoming issues.

Clackamas Literary Review

_____	1 year	$12
_____	2 years	$22
_____	3 years	$32

Name _____

Address _____

City / State / Zip _____

Email _____

Send this form and check or money order to:

Clackamas Literary Review
English Department
Clackamas Community College
19600 Molalla Avenue
Oregon City, Oregon 97045